GIVEN IN MEMORY

OF

FRANCES FRYMOYER

APRIL, 2004

THE HORSESHOE TRILOGIES

Where There's Hope

Read all the books in the first
Horseshoe Trilogy:

Book #1: Keeping Faith
Book #2: Last Hope
Book #3: Sweet Charity

And in the second Horseshoe Trilogy:

Book #4: In Good Faith
Book #5: Where There's Hope

COMING SOON:

Book #6: Charity at Home

THE HORSESHOE TRILOGIES

Where There's Hope

by

Lucy Daniels

HYPERION
New York

Special thanks to Linda Chapman

Text copyright © 2003 by Working Partners Limited
Cover illustration copyright © 2003 by Tristan Elwell

The Horseshoe Trilogies and the Volo colophon are trademarks of
Disney Enterprises, Inc.
Volo® is a registered trademark of Disney Enterprises, Inc.

First U.S. edition, 2003
1 3 5 7 9 10 8 6 4 2

This book is set in 12.5-point Life Roman.
ISBN 0-7868-1748-8
Visit www.volobooks.com

To Jackie Chatwin—for being an inspirational riding instructor and for letting me ride and look after the beautiful, but utterly mad, Sid

CHAPTER ONE

Josie Grace sat deep in the saddle as her horse, Charity, trotted along the riding trail. Shaking her head, Charity chomped at the bit, eager to stretch her legs. "In a minute," Josie soothed the horse, patting her silver-gray neck. As they rounded a bend, the path opened up into a wide grassy track at the side of a cornfield. "Okay, girl." Josie grinned, loosening her hold on Charity's reins. "Let's go!"

Charity surged forward. Crouching low, Josie lost herself in the burst of speed. The wind rushed against her face, sweeping back her wavy, auburn-colored hair. All she could hear was the pounding of

Charity's hooves on the sunbaked ground as the cornfield swept by in a golden blur.

All too soon they reached the end of the field and Josie sat back in the saddle, slowing Charity down. Charity jogged for a few steps before coming to a walk.

"Did you have fun?" Josie asked, stroking the side of Charity's neck.

The horse whickered softly.

Josie smiled. She'd take that as a yes. At the top of the field, Josie and Charity turned down a path that led into a small wood. Charity walked forward eagerly, her hooves lifting easily over the raised tree roots and patches of mud on the shady ground.

Josie ducked under an overhanging branch. "You know we're going to see Hope, don't you, Charity?"

The gray horse snorted in reply.

Josie felt a small twinge of sadness. Once Hope, Charity's mother, would have been with them on this hack. Not just Hope but Faith, their other horse, too. Josie bit her lip at the thought. Until a few months ago, all three horses had belonged to her mom, who had given lessons on them at the riding school she ran. But then the owner of the property had died. Josie and her parents had been forced to move to a new house, and Hope and Faith had been sold. Even though they had gone to great homes, Josie still missed them.

"At least I've still got you," she said, patting Charity. And, she thought, at least Faith and Hope still live close enough that I can see them whenever I want.

Ten minutes later, Josie rode up to a large sprawling house built out of honey-colored stone. Bright red geraniums bloomed brightly on either side of the big front door and a wooden sign said FRIENDSHIP HOUSE.

This is Hope's home, Josie thought. She rode Charity around the side of the building toward the stables. Normally the sound of children's laughter and happy shouts came from the gardens and echoed out through the open windows, but today it was silent.

It must be a changeover day, Josie realized as Charity's hooves crunched loudly on the gravel. Friendship House was a center for handicapped children, who came there for holidays to give their regular caretakers a break. Josie smiled in anticipation of what the new children would think of Hope. I bet they'll love her, she thought.

Hope wasn't the prettiest horse in the world, with her flea-bitten gray coat, small eyes, and straight face, but she was the sweetest-natured horse imaginable. Plus, she was wonderful with the children who came to stay at Friendship House. She would stand still for hours as they groomed her, hugged her, and sat on her back. Josie knew it was the perfect home for her. Best of all, Liz Tallant, the center's manager, had told Josie that she could ride Hope whenever she liked.

Josie patted Charity's neck. "You can say hello to your mom and then I'll put you in one of the stalls while I ride Hope." As Charity rounded the house and came out at the back by the old stable block, Josie shaded her eyes and looked across the field.

Underneath the oak tree were the two dark gray shapes of Jack and Jill, but where was Hope?

Suddenly, Josie gasped in surprise. Hope was being ridden! Someone was cantering the gray horse in a circle at the far end of the field.

Lightly touching her heels to Charity's sides, Josie rode toward the paddock gate. As she got closer she saw that the rider looked about her age—twelve. She's a good rider, Josie thought, noticing how the girl sat lightly in the saddle. Her heels were down and her hands were soft on the reins. Hope slowed to a trot, and the girl patted her.

Seeing her mother, Charity whinnied loudly. At the sound, Hope looked over and neighed back in delight. Her rider looked surprised to see Josie and Charity. As the girl rode over to the gate, Josie saw a hint of wavy blond hair escaping from underneath her helmet.

Josie smiled. "Hi," she called out as the girl and Hope drew near. "I didn't realize anyone was riding Hope today."

The girl frowned. "What's it to you?"

Josie was taken aback by her abrupt tone. "I'm . . . I'm Josie Grace. I used to own Hope."

"Oh, right. Liz said that Hope's old owner visited *occasionally*," the girl sneered. "Well, I'm Zoe Taylor," she said, patting Hope possessively. "I look after Hope now."

"Since when?" Josie said in astonishment.

"Since I got here this weekend," Zoe replied as Hope reached forward and touched noses with

Charity. "I've come to live with my grandmother. She does the cooking here."

"Joan?" Josie said, picturing the capable gray-haired lady who was the Friendship House cook.

"That's right." Zoe nodded. "Liz said that because I'll be here so much, I can take care of Hope and ride her. Of course, I have to help the kids who come here to ride. Sid's about to go away for a few weeks on vacation so it works out just perfectly, doesn't it, girl?" she said, stroking Hope. Hope nuzzled her affectionately.

Josie felt a pang of jealousy. She bit her lip and tried to force the feeling down.

"What are you doing here anyway?" Zoe asked, dismounting.

"I . . . I just came over to see Hope," Josie replied.

"Oh," Zoe said, looking displeased. "Well, I'm just about to take her in. You can't ride her." She clicked her tongue. "Come on, Hope." Opening the gate, she walked right past Charity and without a backward glance headed toward the stable.

Josie sat there, completely stunned. Could Zoe have been any more unfriendly? It was obvious she wanted nothing to do with her. Josie didn't know what to do. She slowly began to turn Charity toward home.

But just then Hope looked over her shoulder and whickered. Josie changed her mind. No, she decided. Why should I leave? She turned Charity after Hope.

Ignoring her, Zoe unsaddled Hope and led her into her stall. Closing the door, she headed toward the tack room with the saddle and bridle.

Hope put her head over the door and looked at Josie. Dismounting, Josie went up to her. Hope lifted her nose and nuzzled Josie in the arm. "Hey, girl," Josie murmured, rubbing Hope's jaw. Charity stepped forward and for one moment, as she stroked both the horses, Josie felt happy. But the happiness didn't last long. Zoe came marching back down the aisle with a dark red sweat sheet over her arm.

"Excuse me," she said coldly.

Josie stepped back. Zoe went into the stall and threw the sheet over Hope's broad back. Standing in the doorway, Josie frowned. Although Hope was cooler now and the sweat on her neck was almost dry, she was still breathing heavily. "She's breathing fast," she said, a note of concern in her voice.

Zoe paused and watched Hope breathing for a

moment. Then she looked at the horse's face. "She's just got a cold," she said briefly. "Look at her nose." She patted Hope. "Let's get you some water, girl."

As Zoe went to fill a water bucket, Josie stroked Hope's face. The horse's nose was running slightly. Still, she wasn't convinced Hope's only problem was a cold.

Zoe offered Hope a little water. "Not too much at once," she told the horse softly. "You don't want to get colic. I'll give you some more in a few minutes."

Josie found herself admitting that, while she was disliking Zoe more by the second, the girl obviously knew how to look after a horse. Feeling a little awkward, she hung back while Zoe put feed in a bucket and offered Hope some more water.

To her surprise, when Zoe put Hope's feed in the stall, the horse nosed around in it uninterestedly for a few moments before moving away. "She's not eating!" Josie exclaimed.

"So?" Zoe retorted.

"But she loves food," Josie told her. "She always finishes her meal."

"No, she doesn't," Zoe frowned. "She only eats half of it."

"I'm telling you, she doesn't," Josie insisted. "She must be ill."

"She isn't ill," Zoe said, looking irritated. "Stop being so ridiculous."

Before Josie could respond, there was a call from the house. "Zoe! The children are here! Can you come up and help?" Josie looked toward the house. Joan, the cook, had come out onto the terrace. Seeing Josie, Joan smiled. "Hi, Josie. I didn't know you were here. Are you coming to meet our new visitors, too?"

Josie nodded.

"I'll be right there, Gran," Zoe called.

Feeling concerned about Hope and angry with Zoe, but not knowing quite what to do, Josie put Charity in the stall next to Hope. She untacked her and made sure she had enough hay. Then giving both horses a final pat, she went into the house.

Friendship House was no longer quiet. Children were milling about and the air was full of voices. Marion and Pete, two of the caretakers who worked at Friendship House, were busy welcoming people. There were several adults pushing wheelchairs. Lots of children held hands, some looked excited and some just appeared bewildered. In the center of the throng Josie caught sight of a slim, young woman with dark hair. It was Liz Tallant.

"Josie! Hi!" Liz said, waving.

Josie made her way over.

Liz smiled. "How are you?"

Before Josie could answer, a little girl flung herself against Liz in a flood of tears. Liz instantly crouched down beside her. "Lily, what's the matter?" she asked, stroking the girl's curly brown hair.

"Want to go home," Lily sobbed, hanging on to Liz. "Want to go home now!" Josie noticed that she had a hearing aid on and looked confused.

"It's okay, sweetheart," said Liz. "I know it's all a bit crazy at the moment but it will quiet down soon. Why don't you come with me and we'll find someone to look after you?"

"Hi there." Hearing Zoe's voice, Josie turned. Zoe hardly even glanced at Josie and Liz. Her attention was focused on the little girl. "Hey," she said gently. "What's your name?"

"It's okay, Zoe . . ." Liz started to say.

Lily interrupted her. "My name's Lily," answered the little girl, looking at Zoe.

"That's a nice name," Zoe replied as she pulled a blue finger-puppet rabbit out of her pocket. "Would you like to meet my rabbit? Her name's Daisy."

Josie watched in astonishment as Zoe made the puppet look as if it was whispering in her ear. "Daisy wants to know if you like animals," she said to the little girl.

Lily nodded.

Zoe held out her hand. "Well, why don't you come with me and we can meet some. There are all sorts of animals here who want to meet you. There are rabbits and guinea pigs and donkeys and even a horse."

"A horse?" Lily said, her eyes wide. She took Zoe's hand. "Can I see the horse?"

"Of course you can," Zoe said, glancing at Liz, who nodded. "Let's go and say hello to her and then we'll find your room."

"Thanks, Zoe," Liz said softly as Zoe led Lily away. She turned to Josie. "So, have you met Zoe yet? She's amazing with the children."

"Uh . . . yes," Josie stammered. She was still reeling from the shock of seeing a totally different

Zoe. The rude, curt person she had met outside was completely different from this person. Zoe had known exactly what to say to Lily.

"She's come to stay with Joan," Liz continued. "She loves horses and I told her she can ride Hope. I hope you don't mind."

What could Josie say? Of course she minded, but Hope wasn't hers anymore. She shook her head.

"Great," Liz said happily. "Maybe you can ride together? Zoe doesn't know anyone around here. It would be nice for her to have a friend."

Josie hesitated. She knew it must be hard coming to a new place to live. But Zoe didn't really seem to want to be friends with her.

Luckily, Liz didn't expect a reply. "I'd better go," she said, looking round. "There's a lot to organize. See you later, Josie."

"Bye," Josie said as Liz hurried off.

An hour later, Josie was riding Charity back across the fields to her house. She hadn't spoken to Zoe again, who had been busy with the children. As Josie was leaving, Zoe had been lifting them one at a time onto Hope's broad, safe back. Hope had looked blissfully happy, surrounded by so many children. But still, Josie couldn't help feeling slightly worried about her. She'd checked Hope's feed and half of it was still left. "I hope she's okay," Josie said to Charity as they walked along the trail. "It's not like Hope to leave food, now is it?"

When she got back home, she told her mom.

Mary Grace leaned against the counter and stirred her mug of tea thoughtfully. "So how much did you say she ate?"

"About half," Josie said, washing her hands in the big white sink and then squeezing past her mom to get to the towel. Their new kitchen wasn't as big as the kitchen in their old house, but it was very cozy with wooden furniture and multicolored mugs hanging up on hooks above the stove.

"Well, you're right, it isn't like Hope to be off her feed," her mom said, grabbing the lid off the cookie jar. Basil, the family's brown-and-white terrier, leaped up from his basket by the door and came trotting to sit at her feet. "Did she look okay otherwise?"

Josie thought of Hope standing happily while the children played around her. "Sure," she said. "I mean, I guess she was breathing heavily after she'd been ridden and she did have a runny nose."

"It's probably just a cold," Mrs. Grace said, offering her a cookie. "Nothing to worry about."

"That's what Zoe said," Josie sighed as she took a bite of chocolate-chip cookie.

Mrs. Grace frowned. "Who's Zoe?"

"Joan's granddaughter," Josie said. She told her mom about Zoe living with Joan and being allowed to ride Hope. "She wasn't very friendly to me," she added.

Mrs. Grace looked at her quickly. "Are you worried she's not taking good care of Hope?"

"No," Josie had to admit. "She seemed to know what she was doing, and she is a beautiful rider."

Mrs. Grace sighed. "Well, in that case I think you're just going to have to get used to her." She put her tea down and placed an arm around Josie's shoulders. "I know it's hard, seeing someone else with Hope. But Hope isn't our horse anymore, and it's not up to us who takes care of her."

"I know," she sighed.

"Look, maybe you just started off on the wrong foot," Mrs. Grace said reasonably. "Zoe might just be shy. Sometimes shy people can seem a bit rude even when they don't mean to."

Josie considered it. Zoe hadn't seemed shy. Still, her mom was usually right about this stuff. "I could go over there tomorrow and see her again," Josie said slowly. "You know, try and make friends."

"That's a good idea," her mom said, smiling.

"Wait! I can't," Josie corrected herself. "I promised I'd go over to Jill's house and help settle Faith back in."

Faith, the oldest of Mrs. Grace's three horses, now belonged to Jill Atterbury. Jill had been in a car accident that had left her with a badly damaged hip. Now she was getting better. She had even started to ride again, but sidesaddle, so that she didn't hurt her hip. Faith had been staying at a local riding school while Jill learned to ride using the sidesaddle. The lessons had been a great success, and Faith was moving back home the next morning.

Mrs. Grace smiled. "I bet Jill's excited to have Faith home again."

"Very," Josie said. Jill loved Faith to bits and, as far as Josie was concerned, if she couldn't have Faith, then Jill's was the next-best place.

"Well then, why not go over to Friendship House later in the week?" Mrs. Grace said.

Josie nodded. She wanted to see Hope again to make sure she was over her cold. "Okay, I will," she promised. "By then Hope will be healthy."

CHAPTER TWO

"Where's Faith?" Jill said anxiously the next morning. She looked down the road for about the twentieth time. "She should be here by now."

Josie, who was sitting on the fence next to Jill, checked her watch. "Sally's only five minutes late. She must have got held up at the stables. Don't worry, Jill. She'll be here soon."

Sally was the owner of Lonsdale Stables, the riding school where Faith had been staying for the past few weeks.

Jill pushed her straight brown hair behind her ears. "I just want Faith home," she fretted. "I really miss being able to see her from my bedroom window. It's strange seeing Midnight by himself without Faith."

Hearing his name, the black gelding who was grazing near Charity looked up. He belonged to Jill's friend, Bev, and usually shared the field with Faith.

"He's been standing by the gate a lot," Jill went on. "He's such a sweet thing. I think he's missed Faith, too."

Just then a red Land Rover pulling a horse trailer turned up the road. "Here she is!" Jill shouted.

Together the girls jumped off the fence and hurried to the side of the road, Jill limping slightly. The Land Rover pulled into the driveway and stopped. "Hi, girls," said Sally, getting out. "Sorry I'm late. Someone called about lessons just as I was leaving."

Inside the trailer, Faith whinnied.

Sally smiled. "Sounds like she's itching to get out. Josie, can you give me a hand with the ramp please?"

"Sure." Josie said, following Sally around to the back of the trailer. Within seconds they had drawn back the metal bolts and lowered the heavy ramp to the ground.

"Faith!" Jill exclaimed. Faith nickered softly and pulled on the lead rope.

Seeing the familiar bay face, Josie felt her heart skip a beat. For a moment all she wanted to do was hurry into the trailer and lead Faith out. But, she held herself back. She had to remember that Faith was Jill's horse now.

Jill opened the smaller door into the trailer. It was obviously difficult for her to climb the step but she managed it. "Hey, sweetie," she said, as Faith nuzzled her. "Can I bring her out?" she asked Sally.

Sally nodded. Jill untied the horse and Faith backed calmly out.

"Hi, beautiful," Josie said, going over and rubbing her white stripe. Faith blew on her hands.

"Oh, Faith, it's so good to have you home," said Jill, putting an arm around the horse's strong neck.

"I'll get the tack out for you," Sally offered. She went into the trailer and came back with the heavy sidesaddle and bridle. "Now, are you going to ride her, or do you want me to take these things up to the house?"

"I wasn't actually going to ride her yet," Jill said. "I thought she might need a few days to settle back in."

Sally laughed. "Faith? She's one of the calmest horses I've ever met." She shook her head. "She'll be just fine if you want to ride her now, Jill. Look at her."

Faith was munching contentedly on a patch of long grass beside the pasture fence. Sally was right. It was as if Faith had never gone away.

Just then, Mr. Atterbury, Jill's dad, came out of the house. "Hello there," he said, smiling at Sally. "I saw the trailer from the house. How was the trip over?"

"Fine," Sally said. "But then again, Faith never makes a big deal about anything. She's a wonderful horse."

"She certainly is," Mr. Atterbury agreed.

Josie and Jill both grinned in delight.

"Well, I'd better be off," Sally said. "Give me a call if you have any questions about riding sidesaddle, Jill."

"I will," Jill replied. "And thanks so much for bringing her back, Sally."

"No problem," Sally replied.

Mr. Atterbury helped Sally put the ramp up and then he, Jill, and Josie waved good-bye to Sally.

"What are you going to do now?" Jill's dad asked her.

"I'm going to ride," she told him. "Sally said it would be all right."

"Well, I'll leave you to it, then," Mr. Atterbury said. "If you need anything, I'll be in the house."

Jill nodded. "Thanks, Dad." Her father smiled and went back to the house.

"Dad and Mom are trying really hard to let me be more independent," she told Josie. "They've been worried about me since the accident, but they're trying really hard not to be overprotective."

While Faith sniffed noses with Midnight and Charity, Josie and Jill set to work grooming her. Soon her tail was silky smooth and her bay coat was shining brightly. "That should do," Jill said, giving the currycomb she had been using a final clean by banging it on the fence. "I'll go get her bridle."

Once the bridle was on, they both heaved the sidesaddle into place. It was much heavier than a normal saddle. Finally, everything was on and the girth was fastened.

Jill mounted. As she took up the reins, Josie

noticed that she was looking slightly nervous. "Are you okay?" she asked.

Jill nodded. "Uh-huh." She played with Faith's long mane. "It's just . . . well, you know what a disaster it was last time I rode Faith here. I could barely get her to trot. What if everything goes wrong again?" She looked at Josie with worried eyes.

"It will be fine," Josie told her. "It was just difficult last time because both you and Faith had never used a sidesaddle before. But now you've both had loads of lessons. You'll be great!"

Looking reassured, Jill urged Faith to a walk. Jill began to ride her in a circle to warm up. She halted a few times, changed direction, and then got Faith to back up. Faith obediently did everything she was asked and gradually Josie saw Jill begin to relax. After fifteen minutes of warming up, Jill tried a canter.

Watching the pair, Josie could almost feel the movement herself. Faith's canter was like being in a comfortable old rocking chair.

After cantering several times in each direction, Jill slowed Faith to a trot and then a walk. She rode over to the gate, her eyes shining. "That was amazing!

Faith is the best horse ever!" she said, enthusiastically patting Faith's neck.

"You two look great out there," Josie said.

"I can't wait to go out on a hack," Jill said excitedly. "Want to come with me sometime?"

"I would love to," Josie said. "Why don't we go out now? I could tack up Charity and we could ride down to the river. It's not far, and I bet Faith would love it."

Jill looked delighted, but then her smile faded. "Wait," she said. "Let me just go ask Dad."

Mr. Atterbury agreed the girls could go out for a short ride, providing they didn't stay out longer than forty minutes. "That really will be enough for one day, sweetheart," he said to Jill. "You don't want to overdo it and make your hip sore again."

Jill nodded sensibly. "We'll be back by eleven," she promised, looking at her watch.

Josie quickly saddled up Charity and the two of them headed off.

"Oh, wow!" Jill said, looking around as they rode down the quiet road that led away from her house and into the woods. "It's great to be out like this."

Josie smiled at her. "Faith looks like she's enjoying it, too." The bay mare was walking eagerly along the road.

A few cars and a tractor passed but Faith behaved just as Josie had known she would. She walked on steadily, her ears barely moving.

"Hey, Josie, have you seen Hope recently?" Jill asked as they turned off the lane and into the woods.

"Yes," Josie replied. "I saw her yesterday."

"Did you get a chance to ride her?"

"No, there's this new girl looking after her," Josie said. "She was riding her when I got to Friendship House."

Jill looked surprised. "I thought Sid the gardener looked after her."

Josie told Jill about Zoe. "She was a bit unfriendly," she finished. "I . . . I . . . I didn't really like her."

"Does Hope like her?" Jill asked.

"Yeah, she does," Josie hesitated. "I guess that's part of the problem," she said with a sudden rush of honesty. "Hope was being super affectionate with her, and I didn't like it."

Jill looked over at her sympathetically. "Did you feel jealous?"

Josie sighed. "I know Hope's not mine anymore, but I still love her and well . . ." she trailed off and stroked Charity's neck, feeling slightly embarrassed.

"You don't want her to love Zoe as much as you," Jill said perceptively.

Josie nodded sadly. "That sounds awful, doesn't it? But yes, I guess it's true. I mean, I don't feel like that with you and Faith," she added. "But I think that's because I like you. It's just Zoe. I didn't get along with her, so it is harder to see Hope being so cute and sweet with her."

"I felt a bit like that when I saw Sam with Marmalade," Jill said. "And I like Sam." Marmalade was Jill's old horse who now lived at Lonsdale Stables. Sam was a little boy who had fallen in love with Marmalade and spent a lot of time looking after the horse.

"Mom says Zoe might seem unfriendly because she's shy or something. And I guess it *must* be difficult for her," Josie said, trying to be fair. "I mean she's come to live with her grandmother, and she doesn't know anyone from around here. I'm going to ride over there tomorrow and try to see if I can make friends with her."

"It's worth a shot," Jill said.

Josie nodded determinedly. "Wish me luck." She looked ahead at the wide path through the trees. "Now, let's get going," she said to Jill with a grin.

After a little while the two girls brought the horses down to a walk. Up ahead there was a small stream that trickled and glistened. Josie and Jill made their way up to it, allowing the horses to get used to the sound and feel of the water. The woods around them were quiet and shady and the only sound was the splashing from the horses playing in the river.

"Charity!" Josie exclaimed as her horse pawed excitedly at the water, sending it spraying up in all directions.

"Oh! Thanks, Charity!" Jill said, rubbing water off her face.

"I'd better take her back onto the shore," said Josie, laughing. "Otherwise she's going to try and roll and I don't really want a bath today!"

They both rode up onto the sun-dappled bank.

Josie glanced at her watch. "Yikes! It's quarter to eleven. We should be getting back or your dad will be worried."

Jill nodded. "You're right, come on. Let's canter back!"

They arrived back at Jill's a few minutes before eleven. Josie helped Jill untack Faith and then she got back on Charity. "I'd better go. I told my mom I'd be home by eleven thirty."

"Come back any time you want to go on a hack," Jill said.

"Try and keep me away!" Josie said as she pointed Charity toward home.

As she rode Charity along the road, she heard a clinking sound. She listened. There it was again. As Charity put her left front hoof down, there was a faint but unmistakable metallic ping. It sounded like Charity had a loose shoe.

Checking that there were no cars coming, Josie halted and dismounted to investigate how loose the shoe was. Picking up Charity's hoof, she wiggled the metal shoe with her hand. To her relief it only moved slightly.

"It's not too bad. We should be able to get home," Josie said to the horse. She remounted and continued her walk home.

Turning down the trail that led back to her house, she tried to work out when the farrier was due out next. Charity had been shod about five weeks ago. That meant he should be coming within the next week.

Just then Charity stopped with a snort. Josie looked quickly ahead to see what was bothering her. The trail dipped down into a hollow that was filled with a large puddle of mud. The overhanging trees had kept it sheltered from the sun so it hadn't dried out like the rest of the path. Beside the mud, the bushes seemed to move slightly.

"Don't be so silly," Josie told Charity. "It's just the wind moving the branches." She touched her heels to Charity's sides. "Walk on."

Charity walked forward cautiously. She wasn't as steady as the older horses when she was out on a hack—particularly when she was out on her own. Reaching the bushes, the horse tensed. "It's all right," Josie cooed, patting her reassuringly. Gathering up her courage, Charity stepped forward into the mud.

At exactly that moment, a young rabbit bounded out from the undergrowth. Spooking violently, Charity leaped out of the mud, her hooves making a loud squelching sound.

Josie lost both her stirrups and grabbed a handful of mane just in time to stop herself from falling off. Charity frantically plunged up the opposite slope.

"Whoa, girl, whoa," Josie said, grabbing the reins. Within a few strides she had regained control and brought Charity to a stop.

"It's all right, girl," Josie soothed, stroking the horse's trembling neck. "It was just a little bunny rabbit."

Charity pulled anxiously at the reins and Josie let her walk on. Slowly Josie felt her start to calm down. Leaning over in the saddle, she took a quick look at Charity's legs to make sure that Charity hadn't kicked herself when she jumped out of the mud. Charity's legs were so covered with mud, it was hard to see if there was any injury. She didn't feel lame but, just to be sure, Josie stopped and dismounted.

Looping the reins over her arm, she ran her hand down Charity's legs one at a time. They all seemed fine. But as Josie finished checking Charity's left front leg, her heart sank. Charity's loose shoe had come off in the mud.

CHAPTER THREE

For the rest of the ride home, Josie rode Charity on the softest bits of the bridle path so as not to hurt her foot. When they turned onto the road that led to her house, Josie dismounted. Running up the stirrups and taking the reins over Charity's head, she led her up to the stable.

Mrs. Grace was outside and came over quickly. "What's happened? Why are you late?" she asked.

"It's okay," Josie said quickly. "We're both fine. Charity just lost a shoe on the way home, so I thought it would be better to walk her."

Her mom looked relieved. "That was sensible. Which shoe?"

Josie pointed to Charity's left front leg. "It came off in some mud." She explained what had happened.

"Poor thing," Mrs. Grace said, stroking Charity's neck. "It must be strange out there without Hope and Faith."

"I think even Faith and Hope would have shied if a rabbit ran out under their hooves," Josie said. She rubbed Charity's nose. "When's the farrier due to come next, Mom?"

"Not for another ten days," her mom replied. "I'll give him a call to see if he can come sooner. Charity will get sore if you ride her without a shoe for too long."

Mrs. Grace disappeared into the house. Josie led Charity to her pasture and untacked her. Her mom came out of the kitchen as she carried the saddle and bridle into the house. "He'll be here on Friday," she said.

"But that's three days away," Josie whined.

"I know, but it's the earliest he can get here," Mrs. Grace told her. "You'll just have to rest Charity till then."

"But I wanted to visit Hope," Josie protested. "I was going to ride over there tomorrow. Do you think you could take me in the car?"

"I'm sorry, honey. My car's going to the shop this

afternoon. I wanted it done before Dad and I went away. . . ." Mrs. Grace was interrupted by the sound of the phone ringing.

"Maybe that's the farrier calling to say he can come sooner!" Josie said with a burst of hope. Dropping her saddle and bridle on the floor, she ran to the phone. "Hello," she said breathlessly.

"Hi! It's me!"

"Anna," Josie sighed, her hopes of the farrier vanishing as she recognized her best friend's bubbly voice.

"Well, don't sound so pleased to hear from me!" Anna teased.

"Sorry," Josie said. "I just thought you might be the farrier."

"The farrier?" Anna echoed in confusion.

"Charity lost a shoe," Josie explained. "I can't ride her until he can come and put another one on, and that's not until Friday. I thought it was him calling back to say he could come sooner."

"Oh, I'm sorry," said Anna sympathetically. "That's a real pain."

"It is," Josie sighed. "The worst part is I really wanted to see Hope. She was off her feed when I saw her yesterday, and now I won't be able to go until Monday. Mom's car's being serviced, so she can't take me."

"My mom could give you a ride," Anna suggested. "She's going over to Friendship House tomorrow."

"That would be perfect!" Josie exclaimed. Lynne Marshall, Anna's mom, ran art classes for the children at Friendship House. "Do you think she'd mind?"

"Don't be silly!" said Anna. "Of course not. Anyway, now that that's settled, how about I tell you why I called?"

"You wanted to speak to me because I'm the bestest friend in the whole wide world," Josie said, feeling ten times better now that she knew she was going to see Hope after all.

"My mom got the day off today," Anna said. "She's going to take me and Ben to that new donkey sanctuary in Weston. So you want to come?"

"Definitely!" Josie said immediately. Weston Donkey sanctuary had opened a few months ago and she had had wanted to see what it was like. "I'll go and ask my mom."

Mrs. Grace gave Josie the go-ahead.

"Great! We'll be over in about fifteen minutes," said Anna. Josie said good-bye and ran upstairs to get changed.

Fifteen minutes later, Anna, Ben, and Lynne Marshall pulled up outside Josie's house. Anna got out and ran to the door, her glossy dark hair bouncing on her shoulders. Josie, who had been watching from the front window, opened the door before Anna even had time to ring the bell.

"Mom said it's fine about tomorrow," Anna said. "I'm going to come too, if that's okay with you."

"Of course," Josie said. "Hope will be excited to see you." She looked over her shoulder. "Bye, Mom!"

Mrs. Grace came outside. "Hold on just a minute," she said. She went over to Lynne Marshall who was sitting in the car with Ben. The two mothers were good friends. "Hi, Lynne. What time do you think you'll be back?"

"Probably around four," Lynne said. "You're welcome to join us," she suggested.

"I'd love to but I've got to go into town to get some sunscreen and clothes," Mrs. Grace said. She and Josie's dad were going away for the weekend, and Josie was going to stay with Anna and Ben. "Next time, though."

"All right," Lynne smiled as Josie and Anna piled into the back of the car.

As Lynne drove off, Ben turned around in the front seat. "Anna says Hope's off her feed," he said, looking concerned. He and Anna looked alike—with their father's olive skin and black hair—but they had very different personalities. While Anna was bubbly and talkative, Ben was more quiet and serious. "What do you think is wrong with her?" he asked.

"She probably just has a cold," Josie replied. "But I just want to make sure."

"If it's okay with you, we'll pick you up at nine tomorrow," Lynne said.

Josie nodded and glanced at Anna. "You'll get a chance to meet Zoe."

"Who's Zoe?" Anna asked in surprise.

"Joan's granddaughter. She's looking after Hope," Josie finished. She told Anna all about her difficult encounter with Zoe. "But I'm going to try harder to be friends with her."

"I don't know why you would. She sounds horrible," Anna said frowning.

"Anna," Lynne said sharply. "That's enough! You haven't even met the girl. Don't be so harsh!" Anna raised her eyebrows at Josie but lapsed into silence.

Weston Donkey Sanctuary was located off a quiet country road. Low white buildings were grouped around a farmyard and behind them there were fields of donkeys. "'Cafeteria, rabbit house, pigsties, go-carts, willow maze,'" Anna read off the big farm map as she, Josie, and Ben waited for Lynne to pay for their tickets.

"This place is not what I imagined. There's loads of things," said Ben. "Not just donkeys."

"Look, there's a pig," Josie said as a black potbellied pig waddled into the yard, its nose to the ground.

Anna went over to it. It looked up at her, snorted, and then put its head back down. "It's disgusting!" she exclaimed.

"Like you!" Ben teased, ducking as his sister aimed a punch at him.

Just then, Lynne came out of the office. "Here you go kids," she said handing them each a sticker to show that they had paid. "Apparently, there's a good

36

place for a picnic just by the donkey foals' field."

"Let's go, then," said Anna. "I'm starving."

Josie looked at the map. "It's just down that way," she said, pointing to a path that led between two barns.

Beyond the farmyard were fields full of donkeys—gray ones, light-brown ones, dark chocolate-colored ones. They all looked happy to be there. By every gate there was a plaque that told each donkey's name and gave some information about their history and why they were at the sanctuary.

"They're so cute!" Josie gasped, looking at their huge fluffy ears and big dark eyes. A gray donkey stuck his head over the fence. Josie scratched his face and he tilted his head to one side, pushing his cheek up against her hand. "You're beautiful," she told him. She read the plaque. The donkey's name was Sam and he had been found half-starved in a tiny field. Next to his history was a picture of him when he had first arrived at the sanctuary. It was hard to believe that the scrawny animal in the photograph was really the same donkey.

"Look, there are the babies!" Anna exclaimed suddenly. "Come on!"

Saying good-bye to the donkey, Josie followed Anna and Ben down the path to a small grassy pasture where three donkeys were grazing with their foals. Beside the pasture was a large, grassy space where some people were already picnicking.

"Oh, wow!" breathed Anna, leaning over the fence and looking at the tiny foals with their long legs and bashful eyes. "Aren't they the cutest things you've ever seen?"

Josie was about to agree when her attention was caught by a tiny chestnut horse with a thick flaxen mane and tail. "Look, it's a . . ." she broke off. She'd been about to say Shetland, but when she looked closer she saw that its body and head were finer than most Shetlands'. "It's a miniature horse!" she exclaimed in delight.

"His name is Peanuts," said Ben, reading a small, wooden sign. "This says he's allowed to roam free because he's very tame and well-behaved."

Josie looked at the donkey foals and then at Peanuts. Just then Peanuts pricked his ears and walked toward her. She went over to him. "Hi, Peanuts," she said. He was so small. His withers were lower than her hips and his tiny, black muzzle could fit in her cupped palm. She had never seen such a little horse.

Ben and Anna joined her.

"He's so sweet," said Anna, ruffling his thick mane.

"You know you are adorable, don't you?" Josie said to Peanuts, who looked at her, mischievous eyes peeking out from under his forelock.

"Picnic time!"

They turned. Lynne had found a space on the grass and spread out a rug. On it were plates of sandwiches, chips, apples, and bottles of lemonade. "Come and eat!" she called.

They said good-bye to Peanuts and hurried over to the picnic.

"This place is cool!" said Anna as she munched on a ham sandwich.

Josie agreed. "The animals look really well cared for."

"You're right, the animals here are certainly loved. So, your mom seems to be looking forward to going away for the weekend," remarked Lynne.

Josie nodded, her mouth full of sandwich. "It's the first time my parents have been away in forever," she replied, swallowing quickly. "When we had the riding school, my mom couldn't go away because of all the horses! I think Dad's really looking forward to it, too."

Anna grinned. "It'll be so much fun having you over for an entire weekend. Particularly with the treasure hunt and everything."

"Treasure hunt?" Josie asked.

Anna's hand flew to her mouth. "I haven't told you? I meant to say something earlier but then I forgot."

"You haven't told her?" Ben said, looking at his sister in astonishment.

"What are you talking about?" Josie demanded.

"Our barn is having a huge treasure hunt on Saturday," Ben explained. "A notice went up this morning. You can ride one of the school horses or you can come on your own."

"And the prize is so unbelievable!" Anna interrupted. "You can either win four free lessons or a forty-dollar gift certificate to spend at the nearest tack shop."

"Wow!" Josie said, her mind racing. Forty dollars! She could buy a new sweat sheet for Charity with that! She had been trying to think of a way to get one of those for ages. But then she thought of a problem. "But how am I going to get Charity over there? It's way too far to ride and Mom and Dad will be away, so they won't be able to trailer Charity."

"Well, I could probably tow the trailer with my car if your parents wouldn't mind," Lynne suggested.

"I'm sure they won't," Josie said gratefully. "Thanks, Lynne."

"I thought we should ask Jill, too," Anna suggested.

"That's perfect!" Josie exclaimed. "I'll give her a call tonight."

"It will be so great if we can all do it together," Anna said, waving her sandwich in the air. "It's going to be tons of fun. There's going to be fifteen things we have to find and . . ."

Ben nudged Josie and motioned at her with his eyes. Josie followed his gaze. Peanuts was walking up behind Anna. His dark, mischievous eyes were fixed on the waving sandwich, but Anna was so busy talking about the treasure hunt that she hadn't even noticed. Josie suppressed a grin.

"I'm going to ride Skylark," Anna went on talking at a mile a minute, oblivious to Peanuts' approach. "And Ben's going to ride Gemini, one of the other school horses. He'd ride Tubber but Tubber's going to a show that day. I bet we have a really good chance of winning. After all, it's not just about riding. To win a treasure hunt you've got to be really observant and . . . oh!" She broke off with a cry, as Peanuts stretched his nose forward and plucked the sandwich out of her waving hand.

Josie, Ben, and Lynne collapsed laughing.

"My sandwich!" Anna exclaimed.

Dark eyes peeking out from underneath his thick forelock, Peanuts looked the picture of innocence as he happily munched on Anna's sandwich.

"That'll teach you to talk so much, Anna," Ben cried.

"You should have seen the look on your face," Josie gasped, holding her sides.

"Oh, honey!" Lynne chuckled, as Anna joined in the gales of laughter. "If you want to win this treasure hunt, you're going to have to be a lot more observant than that!"

CHAPTER
FOUR

"Is that Zoe?" Anna whispered in Josie's ear.

"Yup," Josie replied.

It was the next morning, and they were standing by the barn at Friendship House watching Zoe give rides on Hope. Four children were waiting eagerly with one of the helpers in the shade of an oak tree. Zoe stopped Hope and helped another child climb up onto her back.

"Hope doesn't look too happy, does she?" Josie said thoughtfully.

"Not really," Anna replied, frowning. "She looks a little bit tired, actually."

"Come on," Josie said. "Let's go over."

They walked into the ring. As they opened the gate, Zoe glanced over and saw them. She didn't even try to hide her frown as she continued to walk Hope.

Josie and Anna hurried across the ring. "Hey!" Josie called.

Zoe stopped Hope. "What do you want?" she asked curtly.

"We came to see you and Hope," Josie replied as Hope nuzzled her halfheartedly. "This is my best friend, Anna. Anna, this is Zoe."

Zoe simply glared at Anna.

Josie felt the ring fill with awkward silence. She wanted to be friends with Zoe, and she certainly didn't want to interfere, but she just had to say something about Hope. "Umm, Zoe . . . I noticed that Hope doesn't look very well," she commented tentatively. As if to prove her point, Hope coughed.

"How long has she had a cough?" Anna asked quickly.

"It only just started," Zoe replied defensively. "Anyway, I was about to bring her in. I just wanted to give Lucy a quick ride first."

The little girl riding Hope smiled. She had bright blond hair and big blue eyes. "I love Hope," she said happily. She looked at Josie. "My name's Lucy. What's your name?"

Even though she was mad at Zoe, Josie smiled back. "I'm Josie." Hope coughed again, and Josie stroked her neck. Then Josie turned her attention back to Zoe. "Hope shouldn't be being ridden until a vet sees her," she said.

"It won't hurt her to go around the ring one more time," Zoe replied, glancing over at Lucy's smiling face. "Lucy's been waiting ten minutes for a ride."

Josie didn't want to lecture Zoe in front of Lucy, but Hope's health had to come first. She looked at the little girl. "Hope's not feeling very well, Lucy," she said. "Do you mind if you just ride her back to the oak tree instead of going all the way around the ring?"

Lucy looked concerned. "What's the matter with Hope? Is she going to be okay?"

"She's just got a little cold and isn't feeling well," Josie said, hoping she was right. "Come on, let's take her back to the others."

To Josie's relief, even though Zoe glared at her furiously, she didn't argue. They walked Hope back to the tree where the other children were waiting.

"That was a short ride," Pat, the helper, said in surprise.

"Hope's apparently not feeling well," Zoe explained, flashing Josie an angry look out of the corner of her eye. "Lucy's just going to have a longer ride next time."

The four children gathered around Hope, patting and hugging her. Hope stood as quietly as always but Josie noticed she looked tired and listless.

"Okay, everyone," Pat said. "Let's go inside and let the older girls take Hope back to her stall."

As the children left, Josie turned to Zoe. "Look, I'm really sorry," she said apologetically. "I didn't mean to seem bossy out there. I'm just worried because Hope's clearly not feeling well."

Ignoring her, Zoe started leading Hope back toward her stall.

"Zoe!" Josie called, hurrying after her. "I was only trying to help."

Zoe swung around. "Well, Hope's not your responsibility anymore. She's mine! So why don't you just let me take care of her and mind your own business."

Anger surged through Josie. She bit back the sharp retort that was on the tip of her tongue. Arguing wasn't going to help Hope. "Okay, but she needs to see a vet," she said, trying hard to control her temper.

"Josie's right," Anna added. "Just listen to Hope's cough."

"She's not really sick," Zoe insisted. "It's just a little cold. You don't call the vet out for a measly little cold."

"Well, is she still off her feed?" Josie questioned.

Zoe shrugged. "She eats about half of each feeding. That's not too bad."

"It is for Hope," Josie said through gritted teeth. She turned to Anna. She had wanted to be friends with Zoe but now things had gone too far. "I'm going to get Liz to call the vet," she said firmly. "Are you coming, Anna?"

Anna nodded and, ignoring Zoe's frown, they hurried off.

"So how long has she been coughing?" Dr. Thomas, the vet, asked gruffly as he ran his hands over Hope's body.

"She just started today," Zoe said. Josie shot her a sideways glance. Hope had been coughing the other day when Josie was there.

Dr. Thomas nodded. Although he had come from Larkshill Veterinary Center, the veterinary clinic that Mrs. Grace had always used, he was one of the vets Josie didn't know. When he had arrived he had explained that he was standing in for Colin Chase, one of the center's regular vets.

Hope stood placidly as Dr. Thomas listened to her breathing. "Well, I don't think you need to worry. She's just got a cold," he said briskly. He looked at Liz, who was watching anxiously nearby. "I would just keep an eye on her and that cough. I don't think she needs any medication."

Liz looked relieved. "That's wonderful news. I was really worried when Josie said I should call you."

"What about the fact that she's not eating?" Josie questioned.

The vet raised his eyebrows. "She's going to have to get a lot thinner before you need to worry about that," he joked. He picked up his bag. "Now, I'd better be off. There are other horses waiting for me."

His tone of voice made it sound like he had other cases that were far more urgent than Hope. Josie felt her cheeks redden. She hadn't meant to call him out unnecessarily, but she'd been genuinely worried.

As they walked the vet to his car, Zoe shot her an I-told-you-so look.

Josie looked away.

Anna saw and squeezed her arm. "You did the right thing," she said comfortingly.

"Thanks," Josie muttered, but even Anna's support couldn't make her feel better. Zoe was right. They had called the vet out for nothing. She had made a silly decision that was going to cost Liz money.

"Well, now that we have that sorted out I'd better get back to work," Liz said. "I'm way behind."

"I'm going to see Hope," Zoe said quickly and headed back to the barn.

"I am so embarrassed," Josie groaned as Liz went inside. "There's nothing seriously wrong with Hope. I should never have gotten the vet."

"You shouldn't feel bad," Anna said. "There really could have been something wrong and then, if you hadn't called the vet you would have felt much worse."

"I suppose," Josie sighed. "But you could tell he thought we were just wasting his time."

"Would you stop worrying," Anna commanded. "Now, do you want to go and check on Hope?"

Josie shook her head. "I don't think I can face Zoe right now. So much for making friends with her."

"Forget about it," Anna said. "Let's go and find my mom and see if she needs some help."

They headed to the art room. Lynne was working with a group of eight children making papier-mâché sculptures. The big, airy room echoed with the sounds of laughter, giggles, and squeals as the children plunged their fingers into the buckets full of sloppy, gray wallpaper paste.

"Coming to join in?" Lynne called, seeing Anna and Josie. "I could use a hand." She gasped as a piece of papier-mâché went flying past her ear. Anna and Josie glanced at each other. "Okay," they grinned.

Although it was fun helping the children with their

papier-mâché, Josie was glad when it was time to go home. She still felt embarrassed about making Liz call the vet.

"So how was Zoe today?" Lynne asked as she drove back toward Josie's house. "Did you two become friends?"

"No," Josie admitted. "We didn't."

"She's awful," Anna added.

"Don't be too harsh," Lynne said. "I was talking to Liz today, and she told me Zoe's had a hard time recently."

"Why?" Anna asked curiously.

"Well, she came to live with Joan because her mom wasn't able to look after her anymore. Liz didn't tell me exactly why and I didn't want to pry, but, whatever the reason, it sounds like she's been through a lot." Lynne glanced over her shoulder at them. "I mean, just think about how you would both feel if you'd had to move away from your home and family."

Josie and Anna were silent.

"Exactly," Lynne said softly. "So if I were you, I wouldn't give up on Zoe quite yet."

Josie felt guilty. It was awful to think that Zoe's

mom couldn't look after her anymore. She bit her lip. Maybe Lynne was right and she should give Zoe another chance. She sighed. It was going to take a lot of work to get through to Zoe.

Mr. Grace was vacuuming in the living room when Josie got home and Mrs. Grace was folding some laundry. "Did you have a good time?" her father asked, switching off the vacuum cleaner as Josie came in through the door.

"It was fine," Josie shrugged.

"What happened?" Mrs. Grace asked curiously. "How's Hope?"

"Not great," Josie said and suddenly the truth came rushing out. "She looked sick and she hasn't been eating so I got Liz to call the vet. But when he came he just said she had a cold and now I feel really awful that I wasted everyone's time and money."

"Oh, Josie," her mom said. "If you were worried about Hope then you did the right thing to call the vet. It's far better to be safe than sorry. I'm sure the vet didn't mind coming out. Who was it—Roger Vaughan or Colin Chase?"

"Neither," Josie replied. "It was a new vet.

And . . . well, he didn't seem too impressed that we'd called."

"Don't worry, sweetheart," her dad said, putting an arm around her shoulders. "I'm sure you did the right thing."

"Dad's right," Mrs. Grace said. "I'm very glad to hear that Hope is all right. I don't know if I could have gone away tomorrow if I'd thought she was sick." Mrs. Grace gave Josie a hug and then asked, "How did it go with Zoe?"

"Not great," Josie said. "She didn't want me to call the vet and we just ended up disagreeing again." She thought about what Lynne had said in the car. "But," she added with a determined look, "I'm going to keep trying."

CHAPTER FIVE

Tom Crooke, the farrier, came on Friday morning to shoe Charity.

"That's great, thanks for coming, Tom," Mrs. Grace said as he banged the last nail into Charity's shoe.

"No problem," Tom smiled cheerfully as he straightened up. "I'm just glad you managed to keep at least one of the horses. It wouldn't be the same without a Grace horse to shoe."

"So am I," Josie said, hugging Charity.

"Mary! We should go soon," Mr. Grace called from the house.

"Coming," Mrs. Grace called back.

"I'll be off then," Tom said, packing up his tools and carrying them to his battered, black van. "And don't let that horse go jumping around in any more mud!" he warned with a smile as he shut the door.

"I won't," Josie promised, waving good-bye.

"I'd better go and pack the last few things," Mrs. Grace said, as she headed into the house.

Josie went back to Charity and began sweeping up the pieces of hoof trimming. Usually Basil ran off with them, but her dad had taken him to the kennel that morning because Anna's house only had a tiny yard. It wasn't really suitable for dogs. They had decided Basil would be better off with more room to run at the kennel. Ten minutes later, her mom and dad came out of the house carrying their bags.

"We're all ready to go," Mr. Grace called.

Josie went over to them.

"Now, you are going to be fine, aren't you?" Mrs. Grace said. "You're going to ride Charity over to Jill's to drop off the treasure hunt forms and then . . ."

"I'll come back so Lynne can pick me up at three o'clock," Josie finished for her. "I'll be fine, Mom. Now stop worrying and get going."

Mr. Grace looked up from packing the trunk. "Have a great time at Anna's," he said giving her a hug. "And try not to miss us too much," he teased.

"Have a great time too," Josie told him.

Mrs. Grace kissed Josie good-bye. "You be good now," she said.

"No, I'll be really bad," Josie teased. "Mom, I'm twelve—not six!"

Her mom smiled and got into the car. Josie stood in the driveway and waved them off.

She watched until they had disappeared from sight and then picked up one of Charity's brushes. It suddenly seemed very quiet. She slowly brushed Charity and then tacked up. It was strange to think that she was completely in charge of the house and Charity. She locked everything and set off.

There was a heavy, hot feeling to the August day and, as Josie cantered, she wondered if it was going to storm. "I hope not," she muttered, patting Charity's warm neck. Being out in a storm on a horse was no fun at all. Looking up she saw that the sky was clear with no hint of gray storm clouds. With a sigh of relief, she continued toward Jill's. Twenty minutes later she arrived at the Atterburys.

Jill was just turning Faith out when Josie rode up. Her eyes widened as the two horses whinnied to each other. "Josie! I totally forgot you were coming! I just rode Faith."

"Oh," Josie said, feeling a bit disappointed. "Well, don't worry," she added, shrugging. "I'll ride over to Friendship House instead. Was Faith good?"

"Excellent!" Jill said. "But then again, she always is. Did you bring all the treasure hunt forms with you?" she asked eagerly.

"Of course. Here they are," Josie said. She dismounted and pulled them out of her pocket.

"This is so exciting!" Jill said, taking one of the forms. "I'm glad my mom and dad said I could go."

"If you get some pens, we can fill them out now," Josie suggested.

Jill ran inside and came back with two pens. Using the fence as support the girls filled in the blanks on the forms: rider's name, age, and address, horse's name, contact telephone number, and a place for a parent or guardian's signature. Mrs. Grace had made sure to sign Josie's form the night before.

"Should I keep the forms here?" Jill asked as she

finished. "I can put them in Dad's car so we don't forget them."

"Good idea," Josie said. "It'll be one less thing for me to try and remember."

Jill's dad was borrowing a trailer from Lonsdale, and he had offered to give Josie and Charity a lift with Jill and Faith. It would save Lynne the drive and give the horses company.

"It's going to be so much fun," Jill said enthusiastically. "I can't wait."

"Me neither," Josie smiled. She patted Charity and mounted. "Well, I guess I should be on my way if I'm going to Friendship House. I've got to be back home by three."

"Hey, how's Hope, by the way?" Jill asked.

Josie told her all about the incident with the vet and Zoe's anger. "I didn't go over there yesterday," she finished. "I couldn't face seeing Zoe after everything that happened." She gathered up her reins. "But I guess I can't avoid her forever."

"Good luck," Jill said encouragingly.

"Thanks, I think I'm going to need it," Josie replied as she rode off. She was nervous about seeing Zoe, but she was eager to see Hope again. As

Charity turned onto the bridle path, Josie let her break into a canter.

Arriving at Friendship House, Josie looked out over the field. Jack and Jill, the two donkeys, were grazing happily but Hope was nowhere to be seen. Josie frowned. Where was she?

Alarm flickered through her. Don't be ridiculous, she thought quickly, Zoe's probably just taken her out for a ride. As soon as that thought crossed her mind, she heard the sound of a horse coughing. She quickly looked around. One of the doors in the nearby barn was half open. The coughing was coming from that direction.

Jumping off Charity, Josie looped the reins over her arm and hurried to the door dragging a confused Charity behind her. "Hope!" she shouted in alarm.

Hope was standing in the aisle. Her head was low and her dark eyes were half-closed as she coughed. Zoe was crouching beside her, stroking her face. Hearing Josie, she jumped to her feet.

Josie was too alarmed about Hope to acknowledge the scowl on Zoe's face. "What's the matter with Hope?"

Zoe hesitated, but quickly her concern for Hope overcame her hostility. "I don't know," she said quickly, her eyes full of worry. "I got here half an hour ago, and she was coughing. I brought her in from the field and tried to give her water, but she hasn't gotten better. I was just about to go find Liz and call the vet."

"I'll come with you," Josie said. "Let's go."

She quickly put Charity into one of the spare stalls and together they hurried into the house. When they knocked on the door to Liz's office, there was no reply.

"Are you looking for Liz?" Pat asked, coming down the staircase with a group of children.

"Uh-huh," Josie said quickly. "Do you have any idea where she is?"

"I'm afraid she's not here. She's at a conference on music therapy today," Pat said. "I don't think she's going to be back until tomorrow morning."

Josie and Zoe exchanged worried glances. "What are we going to do?" Josie said.

"Let's go and ask Gran," Zoe answered. "She's probably in the kitchen."

They ran down the corridor to the big, airy

kitchen. Joan was calmly rolling out dough on the kitchen table. She looked up as they ran in. "What's the matter?" she asked, taking one look at their worried faces.

"It's Hope," Zoe said. "She's gotten worse, Gran. We need to call the vet, but Liz isn't here."

Joan looked worried. "Are you positive we need to call him? He was already out here a couple of days ago, and it costs a lot of money to get a vet out to these parts."

"But Hope's gotten worse," Josie said. "We need to do something."

"Will you please call him, Gran?" Zoe asked.

Joan rubbed her forehead. "But I don't know anything about horses. I won't know what to say to him."

"I'll call," Josie volunteered. "I don't mind speaking to him."

"Go ahead," Joan said, looking relieved. "You can use the phone over there."

Josie and Zoe fetched the phone book and dialed the vet's number.

A receptionist answered the phone. "Larkshill Veterinary Center."

"Oh, hello," Josie said, feeling slightly awkward. She'd never phoned the vet before—her mom had always done it. "I'm calling from Friendship House. Um . . . Hope, the horse here, isn't well. Dr. Thomas came out to see her two days ago but she's gotten worse. Can you please send someone out to see her as soon as possible?"

"What's the matter with her?" the woman asked.

"She's coughing very badly," Josie replied.

"Has she got a temperature?"

"I'm not sure—I haven't checked," Josie admitted. "Can the vet just come and take a look at her?"

"Would you say it's an emergency?" the receptionist asked.

Josie hesitated. Was it an emergency? Hope didn't look well but it wasn't like she was colicky. "I . . . I honestly don't know," she admitted

"Well, I'm afraid if it isn't an emergency, then it's going to be impossible to get anyone to you before tomorrow morning. We've already started afternoon surgery, and both vets are very busy."

"But I don't know if it's an emergency or not," Josie said, beginning to feel desperate. "It really could be. Hope is just standing there coughing and she hasn't eaten and she looks so . . . so . . ."

"Okay, just calm down. I'll get Dr. Thomas, and maybe you can have a quick talk with him," the receptionist said. "Can you hold?"

"Yes," Josie said. "I can hold."

"What's going on?" Zoe demanded. "Why is this taking so long?"

Josie covered the mouthpiece of the phone. "The vet's going to come and talk to me," she replied. "Unless it's an emergency, they can't send anyone until tomorrow."

"Well, tell him it's an emergency!" Zoe said.

"Hello," Dr. Thomas's voice sounded at the other end of the phone. He did not sound happy.

"Hi, it's . . . it's Josie Grace here." Josie stammered. "From Friendship House. I was calling about Hope."

"Hope?" said the vet as if he didn't remember.

"The gray horse you came to see on Wednesday. You said she just had a cold."

"Oh, right," the vet said. "Well, what seems to be the problem now?"

"She's gotten worse," Josie replied. "She's

coughing very badly now, and she just doesn't look good."

"Any other *specific* symptoms?" asked Dr. Thomas.

"Well, she's still not eating properly," Josie said looking at Zoe, who nodded. "And her nose is still running."

"Well, it certainly doesn't sound like an emergency," said Dr. Thomas. "I'll book you in for tomorrow morning if you like."

"I know Hope, and I know something's really wrong. Can't you come today?" Josie pleaded.

"No, I'm afraid I can't. There are only two of us on duty, my colleague's out at a farm and I'm here with a scheduled surgery. I'm sure she'll be fine until tomorrow morning. Just keep her warm and let her rest. I'll be there at ten o'clock." The phone went dead. Josie slowly replaced the receiver.

"Well?" Zoe demanded.

"He can't come until tomorrow morning."

"What! Tomorrow! But we need him today!" Zoe said. "I can't believe you didn't tell him that."

"Well, then, call him back and speak to him, if you think you can do better," Josie snapped. She was feeling bad enough as it was. She didn't need Zoe making her feel worse. "He said that it didn't sound like Hope was an emergency. What else could I do?"

"Well, isn't that good news?" Joan put in, smiling with relief. "I'm sure the vet would have come if there had been anything to really worry about. At least this way Liz will be around when he comes."

"I'm going back to the barn," Zoe said tensely.

Josie followed her. "I did *try* to get him to come," she said.

Zoe shot her a sideways look. Her expression made it very clear that she didn't think Josie had tried hard enough.

They stalked back to the barn in silence. Hope hadn't moved from where they had left her. Her head was down and her nose was streaming.

"Oh, you poor thing," Josie said crouching down and stroking Hope's face. Hope nickered feebly and nudged at her hands.

Crooning softly, Josie gently massaged Hope's ears the way she knew the horse liked. After a few moments, Hope sighed and some of the tension seemed to leave her body. "There we are, girl, that's it, just relax," Josie said. "I'm right here."

"I'm going to get her some more hay," muttered Zoe. As she left the stall, Josie saw that she was scowling.

"This is so silly!" Josie muttered. She knew that Zoe was jealous, but she continued to massage Hope's ears. There was no way she was going to stop comforting Hope just because it annoyed Zoe. "She should just grow up," she told Hope angrily.

"Oh yeah, like you're so mature!" Zoe snapped from the barn door.

Josie swung around. She hadn't heard Zoe coming back with the hay. Her cheeks reddened. She was just about to respond when she felt Hope tense up and start another coughing fit. She looked quickly at Zoe. "We're upsetting her by arguing."

Zoe looked worried. The anger left her face. "Hush now, girl," she said, going over and stroking Hope's neck. "It's all right. Don't cough like that. It's going to be okay."

Hope slowly began to relax. Her coughing stopped.

Zoe crouched down beside Josie. The two of them sat there, stroking Hope in silence as the minutes passed.

Half an hour later, Josie glanced at her watch. It was half past two. She was going to have to go if she was to get back in time for Lynne. She looked at Hope. At least the horse hadn't gotten any worse in the past half an hour. In fact, if anything, her breathing seemed a bit more regular and she was coughing less.

"I'm going to have to go," Josie said, standing up. "My mom and dad are away, and I'm staying over at Anna's tonight."

Zoe nodded.

Josie hesitated. She didn't want to ask Zoe a favor but she had no choice. "Look, will you call if Hope gets worse? I'll leave Anna's number in the tack room."

Zoe didn't say anything. Josie looked at her for a few seconds and then gave up. She went into the tack room and scribbled down Anna's number. Then she tacked up Charity and led her out of the barn.

"I'll be back tomorrow morning," she told Zoe.

"Whatever," Zoe replied.

Josie took a deep breath and tried to ignore the urge to yell at Zoe. "I'll see you tomorrow, Hope," she said, intentionally ignoring Zoe's comment. She swung into Charity's saddle and gathered up the reins. Then she stopped and turned, "Zoe, *please* call me if she gets worse," she said.

Zoe's eyes met hers and, for a moment, Josie thought she caught a glimmer of understanding, but then Zoe's face hardened.

"Whatever," she muttered again and turned away.

CHAPTER
SIX

"Oh, poor Hope!" Anna exclaimed when she heard the news.

Josie was sitting on Anna's bed. "It was awful leaving her." An image of Hope, standing in the stall coughing popped into Josie's head. "I've never seen a horse look so sick from a cold." She looked over at Anna. "I just wish my mom was here. She would know what to do. What if it's not just a cold? What if it's something worse? What if she . . ." Her voice trailed off into silence.

Anna sat quietly. "Why don't we look on the Internet? There's got to be tons of stuff on horse illnesses. We could type in Hope's symptoms and see what comes up."

Josie jumped to her feet. "That's a great idea!"

"Come on!" Anna said. "Ben's at a friend's house so he isn't around to bother us with the computer." They ran down the narrow stairs to the study where the computer was kept.

Anna switched it on, and in a few minutes the screen was displaying a search page. "What should I type in?" Anna asked, her fingers poised over the keyboard.

"'Horse,'" Josie said. "And 'cough,' and"—she thought for a moment—"'loss of appetite,' 'runny nose' . . ."

"Runny nose! I doubt that that's the medical term," Anna said with a smile. "What's the proper term for runny nose?"

"I have no idea," Josie replied.

"We could ask my mom," Anna suggested.

"You could ask me what?" Lynne said, popping her head through the doorway.

"Mom! What's another name for a runny nose, you know, the medical name?" Anna asked.

"I guess you could try nasal discharge," Lynne said, coming into the room with a pile of clean laundry in her arms. "Why?"

"We're trying to find out what Hope might have," Anna said. "She's gotten worse."

"Oh, no. Really? Did someone call the vet?" Lynne asked Josie.

"We did, but he's not coming until tomorrow," Josie told her.

"So we are trying to find out the information on our own," said Anna.

"Well, okay, but try not to stay on the Internet too long," Lynne said. "You know it blocks the phone line. No more than half an hour."

Lynne left to put the laundry away.

Anna turned back to the computer, typed in "nasal discharge," and then hit SEARCH.

In a few seconds a long list of possible sites came up. "This one looks good," Josie said, looking at the third site listed.

Anna nodded and clicked on the page. There was a list of infections and diseases that might affect a horse's breathing.

Josie ran her eyes down the page. *Equine Influenza, Equine Rhinovirus, Pneumonia, Bronchopneumonia, Pleurisy . . .*

"Let's go through them one by one," suggested

Anna. "We need to find the illness with symptoms that match Hope's and then we can see what's wrong with her."

After reading about ten sites, Josie sat back in her chair in frustration. "There are so many things Hope could have. It's impossible to narrow it down."

Anna ran her hands through her hair and nodded. "All the illnesses have similar symptoms."

Josie nodded. "She could have almost any of them."

"The only time there are any differences is when the horse gets really sick," Anna said. "It says here that when pneumonia is really bad, the horse's nostrils flare, its breathing becomes labored, and you can see something called a heave line along its sides when it breathes. But when the flu gets worse, the horse develops a distinctive harsh, dry cough. How are we supposed to know the difference between a dry cough and a regular cough?" Anna said, clearly annoyed.

"I guess her cough doesn't sound particularly dry," Josie said thoughtfully.

"At least the vet's coming tomorrow," Anna pointed out. "He'll know exactly what's wrong."

Josie nodded. It was a comfort, but only a small one. Until he came, Hope was still sick, and that thought made Josie miserable.

Just then Lynne knocked on the door. "Half an hour's up. And dinner is ready."

"Okay," Anna answered.

"Hey, can we print out this information?" Josie asked quickly.

Anna pressed PRINT and five pages came whirring out of the printer.

"Did you find anything interesting?" Lynne asked as Josie and Anna sat down in the kitchen.

"Loads," said Anna. "But we still don't have a clue. Hope's symptoms match all these different illnesses. She could have pneumonia or bronchitis or just about anything."

Josie stared at the dinner in front of her. She was never going to be able to eat it.

Lynne looked at her. "Josie, you shouldn't get upset just because of what you've read. Reading all that medical information would make anybody imagine the worst." She glanced at Anna. "Did you bother to look up the common cold?"

Anna shook her head. "I bet if you had, you would have seen that Hope's symptoms fit that as well," smiled Lynne.

"I suppose," Josie said, feeling slightly better.

"But what if it *is* pleurisy or pneumonia or bronchitis, Mom?" Anna persisted "They can be fatal. Hope could die."

Josie paled. Anna had said exactly what she didn't want to hear.

"Anna!" Lynne exclaimed. "Do you *ever* think before you speak?"

Anna's eyes flew to Josie's face. "I'm so sorry, Josie," she gasped. "I didn't mean it like that. Hope's not going to die. She'll . . ."

Just then the phone rang. Anna jumped up and ran to answer it.

As Anna picked up the phone, Lynne put her hand on Josie's shoulder. "Don't worry, Josie," she said softly. "Even if it is something serious, the vet's going to come out tomorrow. He'll know what to do."

"Josie," said Anna.

Josie turned. Anna was looking at her with panic etched on her face. "Zoe's on the phone."

Josie's heart skipped a beat as she took the receiver from Anna. "Hello?"

"Hope . . . Hope's gotten worse." Zoe's voice sounded far away and scared.

"Worse?" Josie whispered. "What do you mean by worse?"

The words rushed out of Zoe in a panic. "Her breathing's much faster and she is all agitated. I called the vet again but he's out on an emergency call and can't come until later. Liz isn't here and Gran doesn't know a thing about horses. Can you please come over? Hope seemed calmer when you were here." Josie realized it must have taken a lot for Zoe to say that. But right now she didn't have time to gloat.

"I'll be right over," Josie said without thinking. Then she remembered she wasn't at home. She glanced quickly at Lynne.

"What's wrong?" asked Lynne.

"Hope's worse," Josie told her as she covered the mouthpiece on the phone. "The vet can't come until later and Zoe wants me to go over. Would you please drive me?" Josie asked. "Hope needs me. She'll calm down if I'm there."

Lynne hesitated, but soon said, "I'll take you over there right now."

Josie took her hand off the receiver and said goodbye to Zoe. She turned to Anna. Anna was already on her feet. "Come on, let's get changed, Josie."

"What about dinner?" asked Lynne.

"No time," Anna replied.

Leaving their food, the girls ran up the stairs. "What did Zoe say?" Anna asked as they pulled on their old jeans.

"That Hope's breathing is faster and she seems agitated," Josie replied. She pulled on a sweatshirt and grabbed the papers they had printed off the Internet. "I'm going to take this stuff. It might help us later."

Josie wasn't sure what was going to help. All she knew was that she wanted to be with Hope.

Zoe was waiting for Josie when they pulled up. "Hope's over here," she called as Josie, Anna, and Lynne hurried into the barn.

Josie followed Zoe to a big stall in the back. Hope was standing in there, her muzzle touching the straw. Her breathing was fast, and with every breath her dark, gray nostrils flared.

"Oh, Hope," Josie whispered in alarm.

Hearing the familiar voice, Hope tried to lift her head, but the effort was too much. Josie hurried into the stall and crouched down beside her head. "There, there, it's all right," she soothed, her hands stroking Hope's face. She knew and loved every line on it, every bump, every tiny scar. "You're going to be all right, Hope," she promised, kissing the horse's forehead.

Zoe had followed Josie into the stall and was learning against the door. Anna and Lynne were standing in the doorway.

"Did the vet say how long he'd be?" Lynne asked.

"No," replied Zoe. "They just said he was out on call and that he'd get here as soon as he could."

"So it could be hours," Josie said, her face falling.

Josie stroked Hope's head over and over again. Hope's breathing continued to be labored but Josie felt her muscles loosen.

"She's glad you're here," Zoe said flatly.

"I'm glad too," Josie murmured, looking at Hope. Then she looked over at Zoe. "Thank you for calling me."

Zoe gave a slight shrug and looked down at the floor. Josie could tell Zoe was feeling scared, too.

* * *

Twenty minutes later Joan came out from the house to check on Zoe. "How's Hope?" she asked, smiling at Josie, Anna, and Lynne.

"No change," replied Josie.

Lynne glanced at her watch. "I'm actually going to have to go and get Ben," she said. "He's at a friend's house and I said I'd pick him up at eight." She glanced at Josie.

"I can't leave Hope," Josie said quickly.

"But I can't leave you here on your own. I promised your mother I'd take care of you. Leaving you in a horse's stall overnight is probably not what she had in mind," said Lynne.

"Don't worry, I'll be here," Joan put in. "Zoe and I are staying here tonight because Liz is away. I can keep an eye on Josie for you."

Josie looked hopefully at Lynne.

"Well . . . I guess that would work," said Lynne. "Thank you, Joan." She took out her cell phone and handed it to Josie. "I'll leave you my cell so you can call and let me know what's happening. And if you need to call the vet."

"I want to stay and help," said Anna.

"I know you're worried, sweetie, but I really think the less fuss Hope has around her the better."

"Your mom's probably right," Josie admitted, even though she wanted Anna to stay. The thought of being there on her own with Zoe was not appealing. But Hope's health had to come first.

Anna hesitated and glanced at Josie. "I guess I'll go home," she said quietly.

Josie smiled at her gratefully. Anna gave her a worried smile back. "I'll call you later," Anna said. She held out the printouts from the Internet. "Do you want these?"

Josie nodded and stood up to take them. "Thanks."

"Call us when the vet gets here," Lynne said. "I'll come and get you later." And, with that, Lynne and Anna left.

"Do you two need anything? A drink, something to eat?" Joan asked. Zoe and Josie shook their heads. "Well, I guess I'll go, then," Joan said. "Come and get me if you need anything."

Zoe nodded and Joan headed back into the house.

The silence between the two girls stretched on.

Focusing on Hope, Josie watched the horse's gray sides move in and out. Then something caught her eye. A line was appearing in the muscles along Hope's side as she breathed out. It started at a point just behind where the girth would go and ran up to the point where her hind legs met her tummy. Josie frowned. She'd never seen anything like it before. And every time Hope breathed out it appeared.

Something stirred in the back of Josie's mind. Hadn't she and Anna read something on the Internet about a line like that? She got up and went over to where Anna had left the printouts. She began shuffling through them.

"What are you doing?" Zoe asked.

"Anna and I looked up this stuff on the Internet about breathing problems," Josie replied, her eyes scanning the top page. "I'm sure one of the illnesses mentioned a line like the one running up Hope's side." She turned the page. "Yes! I knew it!" she exclaimed. "A heave line." She looked at the heading of the section she was reading: PNEUMONIA—CLINICAL SIGNS.

"Oh, no," she whispered in alarm.

"What?" said Zoe. "What's wrong with Hope?"

"I think she might have pneumonia." Josie quickly read over the description. "Listen, it sounds just like Hope," she said. "'A horse with pneumonia will be dull, listless, inappetant'—that means not wanting to eat," she explained. "'It will have a cough, a nasal discharge, and an increased respiratory rate.' That means . . ."

"Breathing faster, I know," Zoe interrupted impatiently. "Go on. What else does it say?"

"'The condition may increase in severity. Signs are a general worsening of the above conditions. As the illness progresses the horse will develop a distinct double expiratory effort or "heave" shown by what is commonly known as a heave line.'"

"That's definitely what she's got!" Zoe shouted. She came and read over Josie's shoulder. "'Pneumonia is a very serious condition. Prompt veterinary attention is required, as the illness may progress rapidly with potentially fatal results,'" she read.

"Fatal!" whispered Josie. Panic surged through her as Hope breathed noisily beside her. "That . . . that means Hope could really die!"

CHAPTER
SEVEN

Josie and Zoe stared at each other. "Maybe we've got it wrong," Josie said quickly. "Maybe she doesn't have pneumonia at all. Maybe we are just making up symptoms to go along with the book."

"But what if she is sick?" Zoe almost shouted. "We need the vet!"

"Should we call him again?" Josie asked.

Zoe nodded and Josie picked up Lynne's cell phone. Josie's heart sank when she heard an answering machine message. She had no choice but to leave a message.

"Hello, this is Zoe Taylor and Josie Grace from Friendship House," Josie said. "We were just wondering when you are coming. We think Hope might have pneumonia. So could you call and let us know when you might be coming? Thanks. The number is . . ." she recited the phone number and then hung up.

"Oh, Hope," Zoe said, stroking Hope's heaving side.

"The vet will be here soon," Josie added.

"Can I see that Internet stuff again?" asked Zoe. Josie gave the pages to her.

"Look, here's a paragraph about treatment," Zoe pointed out, turning the page. "It says that if you can't get a vet right away, that nursing is a really important part of recovery."

"Let me see," Josie said.

Josie read: "'In treating pneumonia, good nursing is of the highest importance. The horse should be kept warm and comfortable on a deep clean bed. Small, easy-to-eat meals, such as bran mash, should be offered at frequent intervals and clean fresh water should be available at all times.'"

"We can do all that!" Josie exclaimed.

"I'll go refill her water bucket," offered Zoe.

"I'll make her a warm mash," Josie replied. As

Zoe carried the water bucket out of the stable, Josie kissed Hope. "I won't be long."

She headed toward the area of the barn where the feed was kept. Josie added two scoops of bran and a handful of barley to a bucket. "I'm going to need some hot water," she said, looking out of the feed room as Zoe carried the bucket of fresh water back to Hope's stall.

"Gran can give you some from the kitchen," said Zoe.

Josie grabbed the bucket and a mixing stick and went to the kitchen. Joan was scrubbing down a table. As soon as she saw Josie she stopped. "How's Hope?"

"Not good," Josie replied. "We think she might have pneumonia."

"Pneumonia!" Joan echoed. "That must be serious." She shook her gray head. "Oh my goodness, I hope the vet gets here soon."

Josie nodded. "Do you think I could have some hot water, please? I'm making Hope a mash."

"Sure. The kettle actually just boiled. How much do you need?"

"Just enough to make it a little wet," Josie said.

She stirred as Joan added the water until all the dry floury-white bran flakes had turned a damp ginger brown.

"Can Hope have a couple of carrots as well?" Joan asked.

"I don't see why not. That would be great," Josie replied, trying to smile.

Joan quickly chopped two carrots into small pieces.

Josie carried the mash back to the barn. Zoe was moving quietly around Hope, cleaning the stall methodically and carefully. As she worked, she shot the horse worried glances. "I'm sure her breathing's faster," she said to Josie.

Josie looked at Hope's sides. They did seem to be moving in and out more quickly. She remembered what the notes had said about pneumonia worsening rapidly. Where was the vet? "Here, Hope," she said crouching by the horse's head with the bucket. "I made you a treat."

Hope made no attempt to eat. Josie dug her fingers into the warm mash. "Come on Hope," she said, offering the horse a handful.

Hope played with the mash, but then she turned

her head away, gently nuzzling Josie's chest.

"I'm going to put some clean straw down," Zoe said abruptly. Throwing the fork on top of the dirty straw in the wheelbarrow, she strode away.

Josie sat there stroking Hope. The sound of the stall door made her look round. Zoe was back, the wheelbarrow filled with clean, golden straw. Without saying a word, Zoe started to spread the straw, making Hope's bed deeper and more comfortable. Dust flew up into the air, and Hope immediately coughed.

"Be careful!" Josie burst out before she could stop herself. She bit her lip as Zoe glared. "I'm sorry," she said quickly. "I know you were being careful."

Shooting her an angry glance, Zoe went back to spreading the straw.

At half past nine, Joan brought them some mugs of hot tomato soup. "Thanks Joan, but I'm really not hungry," Josie muttered.

"Drink it," Joan said, pressing the mug into her hands. "You don't know how long it's going to be until the vet arrives, and you sure aren't going to help Hope by getting all weak and dizzy from lack of food."

Reluctantly, Josie took the mug. "Thanks."

Sipping the warm soup, she felt slightly better. She had just finished when Lynne called. "What's happening?"

Josie explained. "The vet still hasn't come."

"You can't wait all night," Lynne said. "Let's hope he gets there soon."

"Yes," Josie said.

"Are you sure you are all right spending the night there?" Lynne asked.

"I couldn't leave Hope," Josie said. "She needs me."

"I understand," Lynne said. "Your mother would be the same way. I'll check on you in the morning."

"Thanks," Josie said.

When Josie hung up, the phone rang again. A nurse at the clinic called to say that Dr. Thomas had been on his way over when he had gotten a call about a horse with severe colic. It was life and death, but now he was on his way.

"Thank you for calling," Josie said, feeling slightly better.

Just then Joan came into the barn with an armful of blankets and coats. "Looks like we're going to have a barn sleepover."

"Thanks, Gran," Zoe said gratefully as Joan handed her a blanket and a coat. Zoe covered Hope with a lightweight blanket. "She looks like she's getting cold," she explained to Josie.

Josie nodded. The printouts had said to keep Hope warm.

"I'll go back to the house and wait for the vet there," Joan said, and walked out the door.

The two girls sat down in the straw and continued to wait, in silence.

An hour later, the barn door opened.

Josie and Zoe looked at each other, for one moment forgetting their anger. "It's the vet!" Josie said, jumping up. She winced in pain. Her muscles were stiff and cramped from sitting in the straw for so long.

Dr. Thomas appeared at the stall. His face was haggard and he looked irritated. "So, what's the matter here?" he asked. But as soon as he saw Hope, his expression changed. Without waiting for a reply, he hurried forward. "When did she get like this?" he asked, concern now filling his voice.

"Well, she's been getting worse since you saw her," said Zoe. "And then this afternoon her breathing got really fast. That's when we called you."

"She's got a heave line," Josie added, unbuckling Hope's blanket so Dr. Thomas could see. "We think she might have pneumonia."

Dr. Thomas examined Hope's rapidly moving sides. Without saying another word, he undid his bag and took out a stethoscope. Putting one end in his ear he pressed the other to different points on Hope's body. He listened intently, then nodded slightly and straightened up while running his hand over Hope's sides. Then he tapped her chest in vertical and horizontal directions with his fingers. Every time he tapped, he listened.

Moving quickly, he looked at Hope's eyes then lifted her lips to look in her mouth. She coughed, and he stroked her forehead. "There now, girl. You aren't feeling well, are you?"

Josie and Zoe looked at each other in alarm. Josie didn't want to speak in case she disturbed the vet's examination, but she was desperate to know what was wrong. From Zoe's expression, it was clear she felt exactly the same.

Taking out a thermometer, Dr. Thomas moved around to Hope's hindquarters and took her temperature. While he was waiting for a reading, he looked at Josie and Zoe. "Has she been eating?"

"No," Josie replied. "We tried to give her a bran mash a few hours ago, but she wouldn't touch it."

"Drinking?"

"She had a bit of water about an hour ago," Zoe said. "We've been offering it regularly."

"Dr. Thomas? What's the matter with her?" Josie asked.

Dr. Thomas removed the thermometer and read it. His eyes looked grim. "It seems you ladies were right. She's got pneumonia."

Josie looked at Hope. She was scared to ask the question but she had to. "Will she get better?"

"Pneumonia *is* a very serious illness, but with good care she should recover. I'll give her antibiotics and some other drugs to help remove the mucus from her airways and ease her breathing. She'll need very careful nursing—particularly tonight until the drugs start working."

"I can do that," Zoe said quickly.

"Me too," Josie added.

For the first time a smile crossed Dr. Thomas's stern face. "I'm sure she couldn't be in better hands," he said. "If it wasn't for the care and attention that you've obviously given her, the situation could have been a lot worse." He ran a hand through his short, dark hair. "I owe you ladies an apology. I'm afraid that when I spoke to you this afternoon I didn't take your concerns seriously enough. We've been extremely busy for the last few days. But still, I should have listened. I'm sorry."

Josie felt very awkward. "It doesn't matter now," she said.

Zoe nodded. "We just want Hope to get better."

"We all want that," agreed Dr. Thomas, patting Hope. "Let me just go and get the antibiotics from my car."

The injections Dr. Thomas gave Hope seemed to help her slightly, and her breathing slowed. "The drugs I've given her should help relieve her pain and fight the infection," he said as he got into his car.

"She probably won't try to lie down—horses don't like moving when they've got pneumonia. But if she does go down, put some straw around her so that she stays upright. She can't lie on her side because she might damage her lungs. I'll be back in the morning, but don't hesitate to call before then if you think she is getting any worse."

"Thank you so much for coming," said Josie.

Dr. Thomas's pager bleeped. He checked the message. "Looks like it's going to be a long night," he said. "There's a horse having difficulty foaling over at Northgate." He rubbed a hand wearily over his head and drove off.

"So, what are you two going to do?" Joan asked Josie and Zoe.

"Take care of Hope," Zoe replied firmly.

"Together," Josie put in.

Joan sighed. "I guess there's no point arguing with you two. You'll only sneak out if I try and make you go to bed. You can stay with Hope. But wrap up in those blankets. I don't want you getting sick as well. One case of pneumonia is enough."

"Thanks, Gran," said Zoe, giving her a hug. "You're the best."

She and Josie headed back to the barn. Hope hadn't moved.

Josie picked up a blanket and, wrapping it around herself, she sat down by the stall door. She'd never felt so tired before. She yawned and rubbed her hands across her eyes. They were dry and sore.

"If you're tired, you can always go sleep in the house," Zoe commented.

"I'm fine," Josie said. There was no way she was leaving Hope.

A few minutes later Zoe yawned too. Josie thought about making a comment but held her tongue. If they started snapping at each other it would upset Hope. She shifted her shoulders against the stall wall and looked over at the horse. Despite feeling exhausted, she couldn't sleep while Hope was still so sick.

Oh, please, she prayed, as the silence in the stall deepened and the long hours loomed before her. *Please, Hope, you've got to get better.*

CHAPTER EIGHT

Josie and Zoe stayed awake for hours. They took turns offering Hope water, checking her blanket, and massaging her ears. As the bright light of dawn appeared, Hope's breathing began to slow and the two girls fell into an exhausted sleep.

The sound of coughing woke Josie up with a start. Her eyes flew open. For a moment she was utterly confused. Where was she? As she looked around at the stall and Zoe asleep in the corner, the memory of the night before hit her. Her eyes flew to Hope.

The gray horse was breathing quickly and the

skin around her eyes was pinched tight as if she was in pain.

Josie scrambled to her feet. Hope looked as if she had gotten worse again. The noise of Josie getting up, woke Zoe. She looked around vaguely and then realization dawned on her face.

"Is she all right?" she said, anxiously.

"How long have we been sleeping?" Josie said, hurrying to the horse's side.

"Last time I looked it was just before five o'clock," Zoe said.

Josie glanced at her watch. "It's only seven thirty now. We've only been asleep for two and a half hours." She crouched down and stroked Hope's face. "Hush, girl."

"I'll call the vet," Zoe said, picking up the cell phone.

Josie listened to her conversation. It sounded like Dr. Thomas wasn't there. "Dr. Thomas was off-duty, but I spoke to another vet—Dr. Vaughan. He knew about Hope. He's coming over right away."

"Dr. Vaughan's great, and he's really nice," Josie said in relief. Roger Vaughan had often taken care of the horses at Grace's Stables.

Zoe nodded. "He said not to panic. He thinks it's probably just the painkillers wearing off."

Just then she heard the sound of feet on the gravel. Looking over the door, she saw Joan heading toward them with two mugs on a tray. "I've brought you both some hot chocolate," she said. "How was your night? How's Hope?"

"Not good," Josie replied. "We just called the vet again."

"Oh, dear," Joan said, looking at Hope with worried eyes as the girls took their mugs.

Although Josie didn't feel like drinking anything, she sipped the hot chocolate. "Thanks, Joan," she said gratefully. Joan had been so kind and understanding through all of this.

"No problem sweetie," Joan replied. She shook her head. "You should see the two of you. Why don't you quickly go clean up before the vet comes? I'll stay with Hope. There's a new toothbrush out for you, Josie. And don't worry about clothes. Lynne said she'd bring some by this morning."

Lynne! Josie's hand flew to her mouth as she remembered. "I should have called Lynne last night. I told her I would."

"It's all right," said Joan. "I called her. I knew you had other things on your mind. She said she'd be here at nine. Now, go clean yourselves up."

After a night of sitting and worrying, it was almost a relief to be bossed around by Joan. Zoe showed Josie to a small, cozy bedroom just off the kitchen. There was a patchwork quilt on the bed and a blue rug on the wooden floor.

"This is where Gran sleeps when she stays here," Zoe explained. "The bathroom's just through that door. You can use it first if you want."

"Thanks." Josie yawned and went into the bathroom. There was a hairbrush, and a new toothbrush by the sink. As Josie unwrapped the toothbrush, she looked in the mirror. Her face looked pale from lack of sleep and there were dark shadows under her blue eyes. Picking up the hairbrush, she began to brush out the tangles in her wavy, auburn hair. By the time she had brushed her hair, splashed some cold water over her face, and cleaned her teeth, she was feeling much better.

She left the bathroom. Zoe had changed clothes and was sitting at the dressing table, combing bits of straw out of her thick, blond hair.

"I'll see you back at the barn," Josie said.

Zoe nodded and went into the bathroom.

Dr. Vaughan was a tall, thin man with red hair and a soft Scottish accent. Seeing Josie waiting by the barn as he crunched across the gravel, he smiled. "Hello, there, Josie," he said. "So poor old Hope's not feeling well."

"No," Josie said, opening the door for him. "She was getting better last night and then when we woke up a few hours ago she seemed sick again."

Dr. Vaughan followed Josie into the barn. "You must be Zoe, the young lady I spoke to on the phone?" he said when he saw Zoe.

She nodded. "Hello."

He walked up to Hope. She lifted her head slightly and, as he stroked her neck, she nuzzled him weakly. "You are pretty sick, aren't you, girl?" he said softly, his eyes running over her.

He listened to Hope's breathing and heartbeat. "Hmmm . . ." he said, frowning as he pulled the stethoscope down from his ears. "I'm a bit concerned that she isn't responding to the antibiotics. I'm going to give her another shot of a slightly different mixture and some stronger painkillers, as well as a drug called Clenbuterol that will help ease her breathing." He looked seriously at Josie and Zoe. "The next twenty-four hours will be critical. Hope's a fighter, and I'm sure she'll get better, but we need to be certain that the antibiotics we're giving her are the right ones. I'll run some tests on the samples Dr. Thomas took last night and come back later today to see how she's doing. I'm hoping the antibiotics I've just given her will have started to work by then. But call me if she gets noticeably worse."

"We will," Josie said.

"Dr. Thomas said you've been nursing her very well," Dr. Vaughan told the girls "Remember, small meals offered frequently, fresh water, and a clean stall are essential. Has she eaten anything?"

Josie shook her head.

"Well, keep trying," Dr. Vaughan said. "If she starts to eat, it's a sure sign she's feeling better. Try adding some honey to the mash—that might tempt her."

Josie and Zoe both nodded.

He smiled at them. "You two are doing a great job. Keep up the good work."

After Dr. Vaughan left, Josie stood next to Hope. "She's got to get better," she whispered, feeling a wave of despair engulf her as Hope coughed painfully.

"She will," Zoe said determinedly. "I *know* she will."

Josie wished she could share in Zoe's optimism. Negative thoughts kept creeping into her mind. What if Hope didn't get better? What if she got worse and worse? What if the drugs didn't work? She looked down, swallowing hard, determined not to cry.

"Josie?" said Zoe, sounding concerned. "She's got to get better."

Josie looked up and smiled. Just then she heard the sound of voices.

"Anna, slow down!"

"I just want to see how Hope's doing."

Josie jumped to her feet. Lynne and Anna were hurrying across the driveway. "Anna," Josie said, feeling a wave of relief as she saw her friend.

"Josie, how are you—how's Hope?" the words tumbled out of Anna.

"Not much better," Josie sighed, opening the stall door and going out to meet them. "The vet just came again."

"Hi, Josie," Lynne said, giving her a hug. "Ben wanted to come, but I thought that Anna would probably be enough for Hope to cope with. I've brought you some clean clothes. Joan said you stayed out here all night!"

Josie nodded.

Anna looked into the stall. "Oh, Hope," she whispered. She turned back to Josie. "She looks awful."

Josie swallowed and nodded. "I know. The vet's really worried about her. He's coming back later. He said we've got to watch her really carefully for the next twenty-four hours."

"You both look exhausted," Lynne said, looking at Josie and Zoe. "There's no way you can stay out here for the next twenty-four hours."

"We've got to," Josie insisted.

"Not if it's going to make you sick," Lynne told her firmly.

"I'm not going anywhere," Zoe said quickly. "We can't leave Hope."

"Well, why don't you take turns watching her," Lynne suggested. "One of you can go and get some sleep for a few hours while the other one stays out here. Then swap. You'll both feel better." Josie and Zoe looked at each other uncertainly. "You'll never stay awake this evening if you don't," Lynne continued. "Surely it's better that you sleep now than risk both of you falling asleep later tonight."

"I guess you're right," Josie said.

Zoe nodded and looked at Josie. "Do you want to sleep first?"

"No, you can go," Josie said. She wanted to talk to Anna.

"All right," Zoe agreed. "I'll sleep for two hours and then come back."

"Make it four hours," Lynne said. "Then at least your body will have had something like proper rest."

Zoe nodded. She went over to Hope and kissed her nose. "I'll be back soon, Hope, I promise." She glanced at Josie. "Will you come and get me if she gets any worse?"

Josie nodded. Giving Hope one last hug, Zoe left.

"I'll go and see Joan and tell her what's happening," Lynne said. She left the two girls together in the stall.

"You look so tired," Anna said quietly, her usually smiling face serious.

"I am," Josie admitted. She stretched her sore muscles. "But I should get Hope another mash."

"I'll do that," Anna offered. "You rest."

Anna made Hope a mash, adding honey to it just as Dr. Vaughan suggested, but Hope still wouldn't touch it.

"I wish she'd just eat something," Josie said with despair.

"She looks so unhappy," Anna agreed. "Not like our Hope at all."

"I know," Josie agreed. "I don't know what else I can do."

Anna looked at her sympathetically. "Have you called Jill and told her we're not going to the treasure hunt this afternoon?"

With everything that had been happening, Josie had completely forgotten about the treasure hunt. "No. I should have called her yesterday. I totally forgot."

"I'm sure she'll understand," Anna said. "Do you want me to call her now?"

Josie frowned. "Oh, Anna, you don't have to miss the treasure hunt, too. Why don't you go with Jill? She won't go by herself anyway."

Anna started to shake her head. "But you need me here."

"I don't," Josie said. "I mean," she added quickly so as not to offend Anna, "it's great having you here, but in four hours I'm going to go take a nap anyway. You should go to the hunt."

"Well, if you're sure," Anna said, looking worried.

"I'm very sure, and it'll be really good for Jill to go. It'll give her loads of confidence."

"Okay," Anna agreed reluctantly. "Have you still got my mom's cell phone?"

Josie nodded and handed it over. Anna went outside the barn to call Jill and then came back. "It's all set," she said. "Jill sends her love and a big hug for Hope." Her eyes met Josie's. "But if you change your mind and want me here, then promise you'll get me, okay?"

"I promise," Josie agreed. She smiled. "At least

this way you don't have to spend all afternoon talking to Zoe."

Anna sat down beside her. "Is she still bothering you?"

Josie nodded. "She's still not talking to me very much. She seems determined to dislike me. I don't know why."

"It's weird," Anna said frowning. "I mean, you'd think that spending the night here looking after Hope, you would have started to get along."

"No chance of that," Josie sighed. "I don't know what it is going to take."

"Well, I guess you can't be friends with everyone," Anna said, shrugging. "Now, do you want me to dump this old mash?"

"Yes, please," Josie said. She smiled at her friend. "You're the best, Anna."

Anna grinned back. "I know."

The hours went by more quickly with Anna there to talk with. At eleven o'clock, Liz arrived back from her conference. Joan had phoned her and told her about Hope.

"Poor Hope," she said, standing in the doorway.

"I'm so glad you've been here with her, Josie."

"Zoe has too," Josie said, prompted by a sense of fairness. "She's just resting now, and then we're going to swap."

"Do you want me to sit with her for a bit?" Liz offered.

Josie shook her head. Liz loved horses but wasn't very experienced with them. "I'm fine. Thanks though."

"Well, let me know if there's anything I can do," Liz said.

She went inside. At twelve o'clock Anna left to find her mom, promising to check on Charity on her way home.

"She doesn't need a meal or anything," Josie told her. "But could you just see that she's okay for me? I usually see her first thing in the morning."

"No problem," Anna said.

"Good luck at the treasure hunt," Josie told her. "I wish I could go with you."

"Me too." Anna looked up at the gray sky. "Looks like it's going to rain," she said. "Anyway, I'll call you later and fill you in on how things went."

* * *

Zoe came back around lunchtime. She looked better after her nap. Her cheeks had more color, and the circles under her eyes weren't as dark. "How's Hope doing?" she asked anxiously.

"About the same," Josie said, standing up and stretching. She'd been half asleep in the stall and was suddenly aware of how tired she was. She realized that Zoe was looking at her awkwardly. "What's up?"

"Um . . ." Zoe hesitated, her expression unreadable. "Can we talk for a minute?"

Josie was surprised. What did Zoe want to talk to her about? The only thing they talked about was Hope and Zoe could obviously see how that situation was going. She rubbed her aching head. "Zoe, I'm really tired," she sighed. "Can it wait till later?"

Zoe bit her lip. "Yeah, sure," she shrugged.

Josie gave Hope a last pat and walked slowly to the house. Even though her body was tired, her mind was racing. All she could think about was how sick Hope was. What if she didn't get better? Lost in her thoughts, Josie didn't see the group of children exiting the dining room.

"Josie!" It was Lucy, the little girl who had been riding Hope the other day. "How is Hope feeling?" she said, looking concerned.

"Hi, Lucy," Josie said, smiling. "Hope's still pretty sick."

"We've been making her cards," Lucy said. "Can I show you?"

Josie looked at Pat, who nodded. "They're in the family room. When Liz explained to the children about Hope, they wanted to make her something. So Liz did some cards with them."

Lucy took Josie's hand and they went into the airy family room with its comfy chairs and low tables. On the mantelpiece was a row of cards, some of them with glitter glue still drying.

Tears sprang to Josie's eyes as she saw pictures of Hope, some little more than two circles and four straight lines for legs, colored in with glitter glue and crayons. Others were very good pencil and pastel drawings, much better than she could ever have done herself. It looked like almost every child had made a card.

"That's mine," Lucy said proudly, pointing to a card with a simple drawing of a gray horse eating and the message *Get well soon, Hope* written in red marker.

The lump in Josie's throat was unbearable. She bit her lip.

"Did I make you cry?" Lucy said frowning up at her.

"I'm just really impressed with the cards," she said, trying to keep her voice from shaking. She drew in a trembling breath and forced the words out. "It's a beautiful card, Lucy. They all are. I'm sure Hope will love them."

"Can we take them to her?" Lucy asked hopefully.

"Maybe later," Josie said. "Right now she needs to rest." She blinked back her tears and tried to smile. "Come on, let's go and find the others."

CHAPTER
NINE

Josie thought she would never be able to sleep, but as soon as she lay down in the dark room, sleep overcame her. She woke with a start and glanced at the clock by the bed. It was half past three! She'd slept for four and a half hours.

Pushing back the covers she pulled on her jeans and hurried outside. It was raining hard. She ran across the wet gravel, bending her head against the pelting raindrops. The light was on in Hope's stall.

Josie reached the stall door and peered inside. Her heart skipped a beat. Hope was lying down, propped up on either side by a straw bale. Zoe was sitting on one of the bales stroking Hope's neck.

Fingers slipping on the wet bolt, Josie fumbled with the door.

Zoe heard her and looked up.

"When did she lie down?" Josie asked.

"About twenty minutes ago. I was going to come and get you, but I wanted to make sure the bales were holding her up properly first," Zoe explained.

"What about her breathing? Is it any faster?" Josie asked.

Zoe shook her head.

"Dr. Thomas said she'd only go down if she was really weak," Josie remembered. "She must be getting worse."

"Or maybe she's feeling a little better," suggested Zoe. "Dr. Vaughan said the antibiotics would be working by now. Maybe she's not in as much pain, so it doesn't hurt her to lie down."

Josie wished she could believe her. "We should call Dr. Vaughan just in case." She looked around and realized she'd left the cell phone inside. "The phone's back in the bedroom."

"I'll go and get it if you want to stay with Hope," Zoe said. "And I'll make her up another mash as well."

Josie nodded. "Thanks, that would be great." Sitting down on one of the bales, she stroked Hope's shoulder. "Hi, honey. I'm right here."

Hope snorted softly.

As Zoe ran into the rain, Josie looked at Hope. Lying down, Hope looked sicker than ever. Slipping off the bale, she gently lifted Hope's nose onto her knees. Hope's ears flickered and she groaned softly.

"Oh, Hope," she whispered in despair.

Hot tears stung Josie's eyes. "We've had so much fun together, Hope. You've taught me so much." Her voice caught in her throat. "Please don't die. Saying good-bye to you when we had to move was one of the hardest things I've ever had to do. I can't lose you forever. I love you. I need you." Tears trickled down her face. "So many people need you. You've got to fight this. Please, Hope. Please fight . . ."

Josie burst into sobs. She heard a faint sound behind her and she blinked open her eyes and swung around. Zoe was standing in the doorway, a bucket at her feet. Tears were streaming down her cheeks, too. She covered her face with her hands.

"Zoe?" Josie stammered. "I'm sorry, I didn't know you were there."

"She won't die," Zoe sobbed. "She won't."

Josie's own tears dried up in shock. She looked at Zoe not knowing what to say.

"Hope's going to get better. I know she is," Zoe said in a shaky voice. She picked up the bran mash and came over to the horse. Putting the feed down in front of Hope, she sat on one of the bales. She swallowed. "I shouldn't have lost it like that, I'm sorry." She sounded embarrassed. "Giving in like that doesn't help anyone."

Josie stood up and sat down on the bale opposite Zoe. "You're just worried about Hope. We both are. I understand exactly how you're feeling."

"Umm," Zoe murmured. She paused and then looked at Josie. "You know, I had you pegged all wrong."

"What do you mean?" Josie asked.

"When I first met you I thought that you just wanted to tell me what to do with Hope because you had owned her and thought you knew everything. But you really do love her."

"Of course I do!" Josie said. "How could you even think otherwise?"

"I didn't know all the stuff about you having to

move and being forced to sell Hope and your other horse. Gran just told me this morning about your mom's riding school closing. I'm sorry, Josie. I didn't realize what a tough time you've been through."

"That . . . that's okay," Josie said, not knowing exactly what to say.

"It's not. I shouldn't have been so awful." Zoe stroked Hope's neck and spoke in a low voice. "I guess I was just jealous."

"Jealous?" Josie echoed.

Zoe nodded. "You seemed to have everything I'd ever wanted—a beautiful horse, a mom and dad who cared about you, a nice house." She swallowed. "And . . . and you obviously have such a close connection to Hope."

Josie frowned. "So?"

"I wanted her to love me more," Zoe whispered. Her fingers played in Hope's mane. "I've always wanted a horse of my own but we could never afford it, and with Mom . . ." She broke off. "Well, it just wasn't possible. But then I came here and Liz said I could look after Hope. It was the only good thing that had happened to me in ages. I thought Hope would be like my very own horse. And then you came along and acted like you still owned her. I guess I just couldn't handle that."

Josie looked at her curiously. "What did you mean by saying that part about Hope being the only good thing that has ever happened to you?"

Zoe hesitated. "I came to live with Gran because my mom's sick," she said at last. "Not physically sick. She's got severe depression. I know lots of people say they're depressed, but real depression is different. Mom's had it before, but never this badly. She's in the hospital." She stared at Hope's mane. "I've never had to leave her before. We've always gotten through it together. It . . . it was the worst moment of my life when the social worker told me that I couldn't stay with Mom anymore."

"What about your dad?" Josie asked.

"I've never met him." Zoe shrugged. "He left when Mom was pregnant with me, and he's never wanted anything to do with me since."

Josie felt awful. Lynne had told her that Zoe had been through a tough time but this was more than she'd imagined. To have a dad who didn't want to see you and a mom so sick that she couldn't look after you— she couldn't even imagine what that must be like.

"I didn't want to come here," Zoe said. "Mom needs me. I know how to help her, and I hate being away from her. I think that's why I clung on to Hope."

Josie suddenly thought about how patient and calm Zoe was with the children at Friendship House. She knew now that it was probably because she had looked after her mother for so long. She stroked Hope's neck. "Does . . . does your mom like horses, too?"

"Yeah." A sudden smile flashed across Zoe's face and she stroked Hope. "She loves them. She taught me to ride on a friend's horse when I was little. She doesn't ride much herself now. It's too expensive to have lessons and her friend sold her horse. But she visits me at the riding school where I help out—you can muck stalls and groom in exchange for lessons. She loves just hanging around with the horses. I wrote to her and told her about Hope—I sent her some photos, too. I thought they might help her." She bit her lip and Josie could see tears in her eyes.

"Oh, Zoe," she said quietly. "I am so sorry. I feel awful about the things I've said. It's not just your fault we argued. I *was* too bossy. I shouldn't have tried to tell you what to do, but, well, I guess was jealous, too."

"You?" Zoe said, looking at her in surprise. "Why would you be jealous?"

Josie paused. "Because you were taking care of Hope and she seemed to like you so much," she explained. "I know that sounds really selfish." Josie paused, looking anxiously at Zoe to see how she would react. "It's just that I really miss Hope. I'm glad she's got such a good home here, of course, but I still wish she was mine. It was really hard seeing you ride her—especially when I saw how much she liked you." She looked down.

"But Hope loves you," Zoe said in astonishment. "It's obvious. She calms down when you're around. She loves you best."

Josie hesitated, feeling torn. A tiny part of her was pleased to think that Hope loved her best, but she squashed it firmly. She looked at Zoe's bent head. "It's not a competition, Zoe," she said softly. "Hope's got enough love for both of us."

Zoe's eyes met hers, and for a moment they smiled tentatively at each other across Hope's broad back.

Then Hope stirred and lifted her muzzle from the straw.

"Hope!" Zoe gasped.

Hope lifted her head a little higher and looked around.

Josie swiftly crouched down in front of her. "What is it, Hope?"

The horse nuzzled her hands and then lifted her nose to sniff at Zoe's leg.

"She seems perkier," Zoe whispered, as if she couldn't believe it.

Hope stretched her nose toward the bucket of bran mash. "Here you go, girl," Zoe urged, getting up and quickly pulling the bucket close to Hope. "Are you hungry?"

After taking a deep sniff, Hope slowly started eating the bran and apples.

Josie exchanged delighted looks with Zoe.

Hope ate the whole meal. Then, with a contented sigh, she lowered her head and rested it on the straw. Her eyes closed and, to Josie's delight, she looked relaxed.

"She's getting better!" Zoe exclaimed, reaching over and giving Josie a big hug, all anger forgotten.

Outside the sun broke through the gray rain clouds. The threat of rain had passed, and Hope was feeling better.

"This is excellent! Just the progress I'd hoped for." Dr. Vaughan said when he returned at five o'clock.

"She's still breathing kind of quickly though," Josie said, looking at Hope's sides. Hope had gotten back on her feet just before Dr. Vaughan had arrived.

The vet nodded. "That's normal. It will take a few days for her to really get over the infection, but the important thing is that she's started to eat and that her temperature is down."

"So, she'll definitely get better?" Josie asked.

"Yes," Dr. Vaughan said. "She'll need a lengthy course of antibiotics and some tender loving care for the next few weeks but, all that being said, she should be back to normal by the end of the month."

Josie and Zoe exchanged relieved glances.

"You've done an amazing job," Dr. Vaughan said to them. "Hope's a lucky lady to have two such dedicated caretakers. What you need to do now is make sure that, over the next few weeks, she is kept warm and her stall is kept as clean as possible."

"I can do that," Zoe said. She frowned slightly. "What about the children from the house, Dr. Vaughan? When can they see her again?"

"Leave it a few days until her breathing's back to normal, but then small groups can come and visit her. I'm sure she'll love the attention. Although it will be a bit longer before she's ready to go back to full work."

Josie smiled. Relief was washing through her in waves, making her feel almost dizzy. "I'm just glad she's better. I don't care how long it takes."

"Me too," Zoe said, her eyes shining.

"She's a fighter. Aren't you, Hope?" Dr. Vaughan said, rubbing Hope's neck. Hope stepped forward and pulled out a mouthful of hay in reply.

As soon as Dr. Vaughan had gone Josie called Lynne to tell her the good news. To her surprise Anna answered the phone. "I thought you'd be at the treasure hunt," Josie said.

"It was canceled because of the rain," Anna explained. "It poured for about two hours. It was way too wet to go hunting for things, so Sally decided to postpone it. How's Hope?"

"Getting better," Josie said in delight.

"That's great!" Anna cried.

"I know," Josie said. "Zoe and I were really worried about her this afternoon. But then she started eating again, and now she's looking much happier."

"I'm so happy," said Anna warmly.

"Zoe's going to keep an eye on her tonight, but Dr. Vaughan said it will be fine to leave her for now."

"I'll tell Mom," said Anna. "Do you want her to come and get you?"

"Whenever she's ready," Josie said. "I feel exhausted, and I'd really like to go and check on Charity."

"She was okay this morning," Anna assured her. "I saw her just before I went to Lonsdale and gave her some carrots." She paused as if she had just thought of something, "I've just realized, Josie. Now you'll be able to come on the treasure hunt. Sally rescheduled it for two weeks from now!"

"Really?" Josie said. "That's great!"

"Well, not as great as Hope getting better," Anna said. "But it's still pretty good." She laughed. "Now I'm glad it rained!"

"Me too," Josie agreed.

Josie hung up the phone and rubbed her eyes. She was glad she was going to be able to do the treasure hunt, but now all she really wanted to do was sleep. She went to the barn. Zoe was grooming Hope with a soft body brush.

"I thought she might feel better if she had a grooming session," she told Josie.

"Good idea," Josie agreed. She went over to Hope's head and the horse nickered softly. Her eyes looked much brighter now. "I'm going to go home soon," Josie told Hope. "But Zoe will be with you."

"And I'll get you whatever you want," Zoe said patting Hope.

She and Josie smiled at each other.

"You were amazing when Hope was really sick, Zoe," she blurted out. "You were so strong. You always seemed certain she would get better. You never gave up."

"You can't," Zoe said simply. "Not while there's any hope." She looked at the body brush in her hands. "You've got to keep trying."

Her voice was low and Josie suddenly knew that

she wasn't talking just about Hope—she was talking about her mom too. "She'll get better," Josie said softly.

"Yes," Zoe whispered, glancing at her. "She will."

CHAPTER TEN

Hope's condition continued to improve steadily. Over that night and the next day her breathing slowed, she took more interest in her surroundings, and she ate every meal that the girls offered.

"You're going to get fat, my girl!" Josie grinned as Hope nuzzled her on Monday morning.

"Ignore her, Hope," Zoe told the horse, as she threw her some more hay. "You eat as much as you like!"

Josie held the door open as Zoe carried the water bucket out of the stall. "I wish that Hope was strong enough for the treasure hunt next weekend. You could have ridden her in that."

Zoe shrugged. "I guess it would have been fun," she said, emptying the dirty water. "I'm just glad Hope's getting better."

"Me too," Josie agreed. Suddenly, an idea crossed her mind. "You could still enter, though," she said thoughtfully. "You could ride one of the Lonsdale horses."

Zoe looked at her. "Really?"

Josie nodded. "Yes, that's what Anna and Ben are doing. You just have to pay to hire the horse."

"I'll ask Gran," Zoe said, looking excited. "I'd love to go. I've got some money left over from my birthday last month. I could pay with that."

Joan agreed that Zoe could take part in the treasure hunt and even agreed to pay for it as a treat for Zoe. After a quick phone call to Sally at Lonsdale Stables, it was all arranged.

"It'll be great!" Josie said happily as the girls returned to Hope in the barn.

"I can't wait!" Zoe agreed. She glanced at Hope who was watching over her stable door. A worried look suddenly crossed her face. "What if Hope misses me? I'll be gone most of the afternoon."

"Hope will be fine," Josie reassured her. "You

don't mind Zoe going on a treasure hunt for an afternoon, do you, Hope?" Josie asked, stroking the horse's nose.

Hope whickered softly and nudged first Josie and then Zoe with her muzzle.

Josie smiled at Zoe. "I think she saying that she's glad we're friends."

Zoe grinned back. "I'm glad, too."

Later that evening, Josie's mom and dad came back from their weekend away. As soon as she heard what had happened, Mary Grace wanted to go and see Hope.

"Zoe's been looking after her," Josie told her in the car on the way to Friendship House. "She's with her almost every minute of the day. She loves Hope so much."

Her mom looked at her in surprise. "Your attitude's changed a little."

"Yes, I know," Josie said rather shyly. "But things have changed between me and Zoe."

"Well, I'm glad you've worked out your differences," Mrs. Grace smiled. She turned the car into the driveway at Friendship House. "And I'm glad that Zoe was around to help out with the emergency."

They arrived at Friendship House and went straight to the barn. The light was on. Zoe was sitting on the floor, watching Hope eat contentedly. The gray horse's coat was beautifully groomed and her eyes looked bright.

"Hi," Zoe said, getting up in surprise when she saw Josie and Mrs. Grace.

Hope whinnied in delight and pushed her nose into Mrs. Grace's hands.

"Zoe, this is my mom," Josie said. "Mom, this is Zoe."

"Hi, Mrs. Grace," Zoe said. She smiled. "Hope seems really happy to see you."

"Well, I'm pretty happy to see her," Mrs. Grace replied. "She's looking much better than I expected."

"She's improving by the hour," Zoe said. "Dr. Vaughan came by earlier and said she's definitely on the mend now."

Mrs. Grace smiled. "You were obviously in good hands, weren't you, girl?" she said to Hope.

Josie grinned. "The best," she agreed.

"On your marks . . ."

Josie leaned forward slightly in the saddle. Charity pulled at the reins. Glancing to her right, Josie saw that Jill was looking tense but excited. Beside her, Zoe was soothing Toffee, one of the riding school horses. She caught Josie's eye and grinned in anticipation.

"Get set . . ." Sally's voice crackled through the loudspeaker.

The horses, who were standing in a line, tossed their heads and pranced on the spot.

"Go!" Sally shouted.

They were off!

"Good luck!" Anna yelled from the other side of Josie, as Charity leaped forward eagerly.

"You too," Josie called. She swung to her right. "Come on!" she shouted to Jill and Zoe.

Side by side, Faith, Toffee, and Charity cantered across the field, hooves thudding on the golden stubble. When everyone had arrived for the treasure hunt that afternoon, Sally had announced that they must all compete in teams of two or three, just in case anyone got into trouble while they were riding out. Hearing this, Josie had immediately felt awkward. She knew that Anna would want to team up with her, but she had also knew that both Jill and Zoe would feel happier riding with her than with Ben, who they didn't really know at all.

To her relief, Anna had solved the problem. "Skylark and Gemini are really good friends," she said quickly, talking about the horses she and Ben were riding. "So it's probably best if Ben and I make one team and the rest of you go together in another."

Josie felt very grateful. "Thanks," she'd murmured to Anna as they'd led the horses out to the starting line.

"It's okay," Anna replied, giving her friend an understanding glance. "Just don't beat us. I want those riding lessons!"

"And I want that blanket!" Josie grinned. "So let the best horses win!"

Now she leaned forward, urging Charity on faster. "Come on! Let's go into the woods. We can pick up the three different kinds of leaves and an acorn there."

Instead of being a treasure hunt with clues, the Lonsdale hunt involved finding and collecting fifteen different things named on a list. Each team had been given a saddlebag to put their "treasure" in. The first team back with everything was the winner.

Faith, Charity, and Toffee cantered into the woods. "Here, you hold her while I find three different kinds of leaves," Josie said, pulling Charity to a halt and sliding off her back. She threw the reins to Zoe and bent to the ground.

"Look, there are loads of acorns, Josie!" Jill exclaimed. "By that tree stump."

Josie swooped down on the acorns and grabbed one. Finding three different kinds of leaves was easy as well. She handed them to Zoe who put them carefully into the saddlebag.

"What's next?"

Zoe looked at the list. "A white feather." She looked around. "We might find one somewhere here."

"Mmm," Josie replied uncertainly. "We should keep our eyes open. What's next on the list?"

"A brown feather, a red flower, and a piece of sheep's wool."

"The wool's easy," Josie said, putting her foot in

the stirrup and mounting quickly. "We can go to the sheep field on the other side of the wood. There's always loads of wool on the barbed-wire fence there."

They trotted through the woods. Around them they could hear people shouting and calling out as they searched for the treasures they needed.

"This is so much fun!" Zoe said, her eyes shining.

Josie nodded. Charity's neck was already warm, but it was clear all three horses were enjoying themselves. Even calm, quiet Faith was pulling at her bit in excitement.

When they reached the sheep field, the three girls slowed their horses. "I'm glad we're in teams," Jill said as Josie dismounted and collected some wool from the fence. "It would take me forever getting on and off for everything."

"Sidesaddles aren't exactly made for treasure hunts, are they?" Zoe grinned.

"Nope, they're for elegant young ladies," Jill said primly. "Just like me!"

"Not!" Josie added.

Jill giggled as Josie scrambled back on Charity. "Where next?"

"The river," Jill said. "We can get a willow twig there."

Soon they had collected ten of the things they needed—sheep's wool, three different kinds of leaves, an acorn, a black stone, a dandelion, a dog-rose, a willow twig, a red flower, a piece of string, and a brown feather—but they still had a white feather and a picture of a horse to get.

"Where are we going to find these?" Jill said as they stopped halfway up a bridle path. "I mean, a picture of a horse! I guess if we had some paper we could draw one. But what about the white feather?"

"Didn't we pass a big house with a large pond, just where the bridle path started?" Zoe asked.

Josie's eyes widened. "Yes!" She remembered seeing a lot of birds in the pond in front of a large gray stone house. "There's bound to be some white feathers nearby!"

They turned and cantered quickly back down the bridle path. They stopped outside the iron gates. The pond was just on the other side.

"Look, there are some feathers right next to it!" Josie said in excitement.

"We can't exactly ride in and get one though, can we?" Zoe pointed out.

"Wait, I know the people who live here!" Jill exclaimed. "Mr. and Mrs. Thornton are really good friends of my mom and dad. If you hold Faith for me, I'll go and ask them if we can take one."

Jill dismounted and Josie took Faith's reins. As Jill hurried down the path toward the big front door, Josie dismounted to go through the treasure hunt items. She looked up at Zoe. "This is terrific! We've just got one thing left to get." Her forehead creased in a frown. "Though it's not easy. Where are we going to find a picture of a horse?"

"Hmm . . ." Zoe murmured thoughtfully. Suddenly her eyes lit up. "Of course! How can I have been so stupid? I've got some pictures right here!"

"What?" Josie said in amazement. "Where?"

Zoe put her hand in the pocket of her coat and pulled out what looked like six or seven photographs. "They're pictures of Hope with the kids. I brought them to show you. I took them on Friday." She held them out. "We can use one of them."

"Zoe, you're a star!" Josie exclaimed.

Zoe slid off Toffee's back and handed the photos to Josie. "Here, take a look."

Josie took the photos. As she looked through them, she smiled. In each picture Hope was surrounded by happy children.

"I like this one best," Josie said. She held up a close-up of Zoe standing with her arm around Hope. Lucy was sitting on Hope's broad back. Her hands were wrapped in Hope's mane, and there was a huge grin on her face.

"That's my favorite, too," Zoe agreed. "Pat took it." She hesitated. "I thought I might send it to my mom. I . . . I got a letter from her this morning."

"Really?" Josie said eagerly. "What did it say?"

"That she's missing me and that she's really going to try and get well again. She got the first photos I sent her of Hope. She says she looks beautiful." Zoe's face broke into a grin. "It's only a short letter, but it's great that she's written. It means she's starting to get better."

"Oh, Zoe, I'm so happy for you!" Josie exclaimed. She reached out and impulsively hugged her.

Zoe hugged her back. "Thanks."

"It's such good news," Josie said.

Zoe nodded. "I know." When she finally pulled away, Josie saw that her eyes were shining with happy tears.

"We got it!"

Zoe and Josie turned to see Jill rushing toward them. Jill was waving a white feather. "We've got everything we need!" Jill shouted.

As they cantered swiftly through the woods, Jill called to Zoe and Josie. "I wonder if we'll be the first back!"

"We've been quite a while," Josie replied, glancing at her watch. They had been out almost an hour and a half. "But then no one's going to have been able to find everything so quickly."

Turning out of the woods and into the field near the riding school, Josie saw that there were no other horses in sight. "Looks like we're the first!" she said in excitement. "Come on!"

They galloped across the field. Suddenly two horses, a palomino and a bay, came cantering out of a bridle path near to the finish line.

"It's Anna and Ben!" Josie cried to Jill.

Josie, Zoe, and Jill watched Skylark and Gemini fly across the field toward the finish line.

Josie crouched low over Charity's neck. The gray horse's stride quickened. She was catching up with them. Faster and faster she went, her hooves flying across the stubble, but the finish line came just a few seconds too soon. Anna and Ben crossed it first, then Charity, Toffee, and, finally, Faith.

Laughing and gasping for breath the five friends pulled their horses up.

"Oh, wow!" Josie gasped.

"I've never gone so fast!" Jill cried.

"It was awesome," Ben said, his usually serious eyes glowing with excitement. "I thought you were going to catch us, Josie!"

Josie patted Charity's neck over and over again. They might not have won, but Charity had galloped like the wind. "She was so fast!" Josie said breathlessly.

"Like a racehorse," Zoe agreed.

Just then Sally came hurrying over. "That was some finish," she smiled. "But it looked to me as if Anna and Ben got across the line first. Did you collect everything?"

"Every single thing!" Anna said proudly, unbuckling her saddlebag.

"Though the white feather was a nightmare," Ben added. "We found one by the river, in the end."

"We got everything too," Jill said.

While they walked the horses around to cool them off, Sally checked through the saddlebags. "Well, I declare Anna and Ben the winners and Josie, Jill, and Zoe the runners-up," she said. "So Anna and Ben get the choice of four free jumping lessons or the tack shop vouchers. . . ."

"Jumping!" Anna and Ben declared in unison.

"And Josie, Jill, and Zoe each get a new grooming box—containing a body brush, currycomb, dandy brush, and hoof-pick."

"Hurray!" Anna shouted.

Jill looked at Josie with a huge smile on her face. "We all get prizes!"

Josie grinned. Her team might not have won, but she didn't care. Looking around and seeing Anna and Ben talking excitedly with Zoe and Jill, while Faith touched noses with Toffee, Gemini, and Skylark, she felt a warm glow spread through her right down to her toes. Her friends were all happy, and Hope was finally well again. It was the best feeling in the world!